CW00493284

Searching For Her Boys: A Search For Hope

Tenise Cook

Published by Tenise Cook, 2024.

This is a work of fiction. Similarities to real people, places, or events are entirely coincidental.

SEARCHING FOR HER BOYS: A SEARCH FOR HOPE

First edition. April 1, 2024.

Copyright © 2024 Tenise Cook.

ISBN: 979-8223774464

Written by Tenise Cook.

To my grandmother whom I never met but feel like I know--Thank you for whispering in my ear all these years to keep fighting and for helping me to give you a voice.

Dedicated to all the women who came before me that fought to chip away at generational cycles and helped create the woman I am today. May your stories of courage and resilience continue on through the next generations to come.

Special Acknowledgment to Melinda Flanagan for being my Editor in Chief.

Chapter One- (Daisy)

Mama was a bigger than life kind of woman. She stuck out everywhere she went with her long legs and perfect body. She had a smile that could knock a man down to his knees. Her flawless skin was soft and golden. She had dark hair that she kept in big curls that draped just over her shoulders. Deep red was the color she always chose to put on her lips and her eyes were such a deep brown they could swallow you right up. She was never seen in anything but a pretty dress or mini skirt and heels, oh, how she loved her heels.

"A girl's gotta look classy, Daisy.", she'd say as she'd swing her hips in the mirror, walking back and forth to check that she looked just right. This woman was mesmerizing. She could get any man she wanted with the click of those heels she wore.

On the outside she was strong and confident, taking "no crap from nobody", she often would say.

But, if you searched her soul you would find that hiding under all that sass was a woman in distress, searching for something.

Mama and I found ourselves at my Nanny's house one night after she'd had enough of my father's "tough love", as he called it. He'd hit her again, this time bruising her eye and causing her nose to bleed. I was standing next to her in the kitchen when it happened. It's all a blur and a very faded memory since I was only four years old, but what I do remember of it was fear.

She yelled at him, crying hysterically, "That's it Mike! I can't do this anymore!".

Quickly, she picked me up and whisked me away out the door.

As she began out the door she stopped for a moment. Looking behind her she said, "I'll be back in the morning to get the boys.".

He stumbled to the door after us, hollering in a drunken slur, "If you leave now, you'll never see them again!".

As she pushed my tiny body into the car she spoke to him one more time, "I'll be back for them in the morning!", she yelled back as she quickly got into the car, slamming the door. As we backed out of the driveway, he came running towards the car wearing nothing but his boxers.

"Mabel!", he yelled, "You whore!".

With that, she put the car in drive and sped away.

She cried as she drove, speeding through dark streets to safety at Nanny's.

I crawled over beside her in the front seat and put my head on her side, trying my best to comfort her.

That's about all I remember of that night.

From there on tiny pieces of how it all happened still sit in my memory.

We were a family of six, me being the baby. My Dad, Mike Mair, was a very slim man with a pointy nose and dark hair slicked to the side. I never felt like he cared for me much in the little time I was around him as a child. He seemed very proud of my three older brothers, Matt, Marc and Mitch, though, who weren't much older than me.

At the time, Matt, my oldest brother, was eight. He helped Mama with Mitch and I, especially when Marc, whom she called "strong willed", gave her fits.

Matt was the only one of us with golden blonde hair, but he looked the most like Daddy, tall and skinny with a pointy nose and deep set brown eyes. Most days, he'd help me put my shoes on, "Okay Daisy, this shoe goes on this foot.", showing me which foot to put into which shoe, "You ready?", he'd say after buckling both shoes. I'd nod my head and he'd walk with me down the hall of our house and into the living area. Most mornings he'd sit with me on the couch and watch morning cartoons while Mama was in the kitchen making breakfast. I loved it when school was out for summer break. It meant mornings with Matt while Marc and Mitch slept in. He was my protector when Daddy was around. As soon as he got home from work, Matt would help me get back outside to play before Daddy even came in the house. I never understood why Daddy didn't call me by my name, just "that one" or "girl". Matt always called me by my name and he said it as if it were the most beautiful name in the world, "Daisy".

When it was time to do something or go somewhere Daddy would say, "Matt, get the girl.", or "Matt get that one inside.". Matt would nod and then say, "Come on, Daisy, it's time to eat.", or "Daisy, it's time to go inside.". Sometimes he'd carry me, but most of the time he'd hold my hand. With Matt, I felt important and safe.

Marc and Mitch were my best playmates, my only playmates. Together we'd build forts with Lincoln Logs or play with their old toy cars and trucks outside. I had a doll, but most of the time I chose to play with my brothers' toys. I slept with my doll and carried it around the house playing with it from time to time, but it wasn't the same as playing with my brothers. They were the ones who helped bring things to life in our imaginary worlds. Without them, my doll was just a doll.

Marc was six and as Daddy said, "hell on wheels". He was the one everyone else saw as the handsome one. His eyes were a deep brown and he had the longest eyelashes I'd ever seen on a boy. His skin was more golden than the rest of us and he had deep dimples in his cheeks just like Mama.

Mitch was five, just a year older than me. He didn't talk much and mostly spent his time following Marc around. Marc could talk Mitch into just about anything so, he usually got into trouble right along with Marc. He and Marc were inseparable, people always mistook them for twins although they didn't look much alike. Mitch was a chubby little boy with Daddy's deep set dark brown eyes and also a little bit of the same pointy nose that was just starting to form as his baby face was beginning to shed.

His hair was lighter brown, wispy and thin too, while Marc had a slight curl to his hair.

Mama loved having all of us kids. She made sure that Matt and Marc looked nice and clean for school. She'd comb their hair just like Daddy's, slicked over to the side.

She made every meal at home, but our favorite one was breakfast. This was the meal we had everyday just after Daddy had left for work so it always felt more relaxed than supper time. She would sit at the table to eat with us and laugh at our silliness, sing along to our nursery rhymes and talk about what our day would hold.

It always felt like we had two mothers in one, the daytime Mama and the evening Mama.

The daytime Mama went outside to sit on the porch and watch us play, sometimes getting involved in a game of hide and seek or ring-around-the-rosie. She loved to take us for walks and would point out things she saw and telling us a little about it, "Oh, that's an evergreen.", she'd stop by a tree on our walk to touch the needles, "They stay green all year long and never lose their leaves.", she'd inform us.

"Ev-green", Mitch repeated as he touched the needles of the tree with her.

Mama loved art and would color with us in the living area. She could draw anything we asked her to and it always seemed to come to life on the paper. We especially liked it when she drew animals and then made its sound, "Oink, oink, oink", drawing a pig, "What color do we want the pig to be?", she'd ask us.

"Red!", Mitch would say, he always chose red for everything. Mama would giggle and color the pig red, "Red pig, red pig, oink, oink, oink.", she'd sing.

Even while entertaining us throughout the day she always made sure to have the chores done before Daddy got home and we knew when he was about to be home. That's when evening began and another side of Mama would come out.

A nervous woman who went around the house making sure everything was picked up and straightened. Anxious to get any clothes put away and start supper.

She almost always had supper ready as soon as he walked in the door.

He'd come in, dressed in blue coveralls with his name written on a patch that was ironed to the front, carrying a black metal lunchbox that Mama packed for him every morning. He'd sniff the air when he came in, asking, "What are we having?". Mama would call out the short menu from the kitchen and then he'd go change out of his work clothes. When he'd come back, he'd sit down in a chair at the table and wait for Mama to place his plate full of food in front of him.

Mama would call for us kids to join them at the table where she'd have our plates ready for us to sit and eat. Daddy didn't say much at the table except, "Stop that." or "Chew with your mouth closed.". He'd roll his eyes and huff at our every movement that he felt needed correction. As soon as he was finished eating he was gone from the table as quickly as he had sat down. Without a word, he would go outside to fiddle with his car or sit in his big chair beside the couch and read the newspaper. Most of the evening was spent tip-toeing around the house so as not to disturb him.

Mama did her best to keep me and my brothers content and out of Daddy's way.

The night we went to Nanny's had been like any other night until Daddy got mad. I'd seen him get upset with Mama before so when he started yelling at her I knew the routine and most of the time we ended up at Nanny's. Only this time she left the boys behind in their beds.

Chapter Two- (Matt)

I'd heard them arguing that night, same as most nights. I was pretending to be asleep with my two younger brothers. My baby sister, Daisy, had gotten up out of bed again and I could hear her small voice hollering for Dad to stop. Of course, her voice was being drowned out by all the yelling. Then I heard him hit her, I knew the sound of skin slapping skin too well.

She'd had enough is what she told him. It was something I'd heard her say many times before. She told him she was leaving for good this time.

Dad laughed, "Go ahead, you whore, you'll be back as soon as you need money.", he said with his voice raised. My heart was screaming to her as I heard her and a crying Daisy going out the door, it was shouting, "Mama! Take me with you!".

I jumped up and crawled to the edge of my bed to peek out of the blinds. She was putting Daisy in the car as Dad was following after her.

All at the same time, I silently cheered for her to make it out while also having an intense feeling that I may never see her again this time. It wasn't like her to leave without us boys too.

As I heard Dad come back into the house, I hurried to lay back down. I could hear him stumbling down the hall, bouncing back and forth from wall to wall, past my bedroom I shared with my brothers.

He was mumbling as he passed by, calling Mama names and swearing she'd never see us again.

Us boys were close in age, only a year and a half between each of us. I was the oldest and at the time, eight. Our parents gave us all names that began with M just like theirs, Mike and Mabel, as well as, our last name, Mair

Matt was my name, Marc and Mitch were my brothers.

Mike Mair wasn't very tall, only about 5 '7, he preferred to stand up as straight as possible to make himself seem taller. He was a thin man who always wore a couple of layers to seem heavier than he was too. It was as if he was a walking mirage of what he wished he was. His hair was dark brown and always slicked to the side. He had a long, pointy nose and deep set, deceiving brown eyes.

His drinking had begun just before Daisy was born. Mama had always dreamed of having a girl named Daisy, so when she came home with her, we weren't surprised that Daisy wasn't given the name Mona like Dad had wanted.

From the moment Mama walked in the door with that baby girl, until the night they sped away, Dad refused to accept Daisy as his child.

In fact, most of their arguments were about Dad thinking Mama was with other men while he was at work.

I never understood why he thought that since I'd never seen her with anyone but Dad or us kids. Mama consistently denied it, telling him he was crazy, but he just didn't believe her. The more he drank, the more obsessed about it he got. It had gotten to the point that he wouldn't even look at Daisy or call her by her name, instead calling her, "that one".

That night as I laid there, I heard Dad fall into his bed. I closed my eyes hoping to see Mama in the morning.

I imagined waking up to her in the kitchen, with the smell of bacon and eggs in the air. She'd be wearing her white apron with red polka-dots, the spatula in one hand turning to say, "Good mornin' sunshine.", smiling, "What'll it be?". As I longed for her I drifted to sleep.

When I woke up the next morning, I sat straight up in bed. Looking around I saw that my brothers had already woken and were out of the room.

I got up and walked down the hall towards the living room, hoping to smell breakfast.

Marc and Mitch were busy building forts on the floor with their Lincoln logs.

There were no smells of bacon or eggs. No sounds of pans being shuffled.

Peering into the kitchen, there was no sign of Mama.

I plopped onto the couch and looked around. Maybe Mama came back while I was asleep. Maybe she's in bed., I thought.

"Stop it, Mitch! That's mine!", Marc called out as he began to wrestle a Lincoln log from Mitch's hand. The two began arguing as I sat wondering about Mama.

"Would you two stop fighting!", Dad's voice came from down the hall. As he entered the room still only in his boxers he walked over to the boys and firmly patted the backs of their heads.

He walked into the kitchen as if looking for something, moving piles of bills around that had been sitting on the counter.

He found a pen, tore off a piece of an envelope and scribbled something down.

"Matthew?", he called to me.

"Sir?", I answered.

"Run on into your room and get dressed.", he walked back through the living room, stepping over the Lincoln logs on the floor.

"Marcus, you too.", he said behind him as he walked down the hall, "And find something for Mitchie.".

I got up and went to the bedroom. Opening the drawer, I found all of my neatly folded clothes that had been placed there by Mama. She always picked my clothes out for the day so I wasn't really sure what to get out. I chose some jeans with holes in the knees that Mama never let me wear to school and a white t-shirt.

After I was dressed I helped Mitch find something to wear while Marc got himself dressed.

"Where's Mama?", Mitch asked me as I helped him zip his pants.

"I'm not sure. Maybe at Nanny's.", I answered.

I hoped she was at Nanny's anyway and that maybe we were getting dressed to go get her.

Usually, when these fights between Mama and Dad happened in the past, Dad would pull up in Nanny's driveway one morning. After a few days of Mama hiding us out in Nanny's house he'd come to the door and ask to see Mama. She'd go out to talk to him and he'd tell her how sorry he was this time. They'd stay out there a while until Mama would come back in and tell Nanny we were going back home.

There wasn't much to imagine about it all. The only difference this time was that this time we weren't at Nanny's with her. This was the first time she had left us behind taking only Daisy. It could only have been because we were already in bed since I heard her tell Dad she'd be back for us.

Dad came into the room now dressed in one of his many white button up shirts with a pocket on the front he used to hold his cigarettes. His hair slicked to the side, he slipped on his jacket, nodded at us and said, "Alright, let's go.".

Maybe Dad will drop us off with them this time, I thought. I couldn't wait to see her.

As we drove we went a different way than the way to Nanny's.

Nanny lived outside of town on a dirt road but we were going somewhere downtown.

We pulled up to an office building with lots of names on the front windows.

"You boys stay right here.", Dad said as he rolled down the windows and then got out of the car.

He slid his hand over his hair to smooth it out, tucked his shirt into his pants and went inside.

Marc began kicking the back of the front car seat as Mitch stood up and climbed in front. I stayed right where I was, gazing out the window and wondering about Mama.

I was hoping whatever Dad was doing in that office wouldn't take long so we could get to her soon.

Chapter Three- (Daisy)

Nanny lived outside of town in a small cottage type house. It was set far back in the woods off a dirt road.

Nanny wasn't your average grandmother. She was loud with a voice that carried all the way down the street and a chuckle that most of the time got carried away. She was thin and beautiful with curly, short hair that framed her pug nosed face. She usually smelled like cinnamon and cigarettes and always wore a dress unless she was working out in the shed in her forest of a backyard. That was when you'd see her in a pair of worn out coveralls and some old work gloves. The shed was large and painted red with white trim just like the barns I had seen in books. You could find her in there creating all kinds of things from whatever scraps of metal or wood she'd found lying around. My favorite piece was a windchime that hung right outside of her front door. It was made from different items like spoons, screws, nails, nuts and bolts, with an old piece of a windmill on top. I loved her imagination and how she could turn something useless into a working piece of art. She had old tires around the outside of her house that were used for different types of plants and flowers including a big tractor tire in the backyard filled with sand for us kids to play in when we came over.

"Nothing's useless, Daisy.", she'd say, "It just has to find its potential.".
Her first love was men, she'd been married so many times I wasn't really sure which one of her husbands was my grandfather. It seemed like she had a new boyfriend every year and her way of picking them was passed down to Mama. One of them stole some money she'd been hiding. She always tucked money into random places around her house. Anytime Mama needed a little cash Nanny would go looking in odd places, under mattresses, in old coffee cans, holes in the back of cabinets, one time there was a pair of old work boots she kept at her

front door that had a hundred dollar bill tucked inside the toe. One day, that man who stole from her had figured out her hiding spots and scavenged around her whole house finding money in all of her spots. We had come to visit that time and found her searching the house to find all of the places she'd hid money were empty.

"No, no, no!", she cried each time she found another empty place. She wandered through the house picking up wicker baskets and looking behind knick knacks, coming away empty handed each time until finally, putting her finger in the air, "One more place!", she said hopefully, as she ran down the hall to her guest bedroom and opened up the closet. She swung through coats that had been hanging in there and pulled out her vacuum and a bag that held her beloved bowling ball. Getting down on her hands and knees she pulled up a piece of carpet on the floor of the closet where underneath was a small plank with a hook. She pulled it up and reached in. I remember Mama asking, "Oh, Mom, why do you do this? Why won't you just use the bank?".

As Nanny raised up off the floor she held up a wad of hundred dollar bills, "Banks are like men, Mabel.", she answered, "They'll steal everything you've got and then some.".

Tucking some of the money she had revealed to us in her bra, she put the rest back into the hiding spot and covered it all back up, replacing the carpet, bowling ball and vacuum, "Never trust any of 'em.", she added.

Her second love was lipstick. Just like Mama, she had every shade she could get her hands on and never went anywhere without a few sticks in her purse.

She'd dab some onto her lips, look into the mirror, smack her lips together and be ready to go anywhere.

This time, when we got to her house after leaving our house in a hurry, it was dark as Mama carried me up to the door and knocked frantically, calling for her mother from outside, "Mom! Mom, it's me, Mabel, please open the door!", she hollered, peeking in the window next to the front door.

We heard footsteps coming from inside the house as lights began turning on one at a time throughout the house.

There was a jiggle on the doorknob from inside and then the sound of the deadbolt being unlocked, then the chain lock and last the lock on the doorknob.

Nanny poked her head through the crack of the door as she opened it, holding her robe closed, "Oh, Mabel, come on in.", she said as she opened the door for us. After tying her robe, she grabbed me from Mama's arms and put her arm around Mama, embracing her. That's when Mama melted and began crying, "Oh, Mom, he's done it again.".

"Shhhhh, it's alright now.", Nanny said as she guided Mama to a chair in the kitchen.

She carried me back to the living room and laid me on the couch, stroking my face and pushing my hair back, she covered me with a blanket.

Then, Nanny went back to the kitchen to tend to Mama.

"What'd he do this time?", she asked Mama as she started a pot of coffee and opened the icebox. Reaching in, she pulled out a steak wrapped in plastic. She grabbed a rag from a drawer to wet in the sink and then began dabbing it on Mama's face. She wiped the blood from her nose and then put the steak on her eye, "Here, hold this right there.", she told Mama.

"He's at it again.", she began, "He swore he wouldn't do this again. He was drinking tonight as I was cleaning up the kitchen. He found a piece of paper with a number written on it. It was the number for the plumber so he could come look at the sink.".

As Nanny was wringing out another wet rag she listened intently to Mama.

"He came into the kitchen with it and spun me around and waved it in my face asking me who was Pete.", Mama whimpered as she told her story.

"Well, did you tell him?", Nanny asked.

"Yeah, well at first I didn't know who he was talking about. So I asked him, I said, 'Pete? I don't know.'. That's when he slapped me and shoved the paper in my face. He said, ' Oh, you don't know, huh? Let me help jog your memory.'. And then he hit me again, making my nose bleed.".

"That bastard.", Nanny started, "And so, did you tell him?".

"Yes, I looked at the paper and told him, I said, 'Pete's the plumber.', then he shoved the paper as hard as he could into my face and mocked me, he said, 'Ohhh, Pete's the plumber.'. He batted his eyes and held his hands to his chest and then he started opening up the cabinet under the sink.", Mama started crying again.

Nanny dabbed the second wet rag on Mama's forehead and then laid it on the back of her neck as Mama continued.

"Then he said, 'Ohhh you need your pipes worked on again, huh?', and he started yanking out everything under the sink and throwing it in the kitchen.

I told him to stop and listen but he just kept going. Daisy woke up and came in and hid behind me. He stopped for a minute and stood up as close as he could to me and talked through his teeth, 'Tell me, Mabel, is this Pete the plumber your bastard child's father?', and that's when I tried to push him away.".

"Oh? Good girl, and then what did he do?", Nanny asked as she poured each of them some coffee, handing Mama a cup. She sat at the table with Mama and sipped slowly as she kept listening.

"Well, I pushed him and then he kept coming back into my face, so I pushed him again and tried walking past him to go get the boys but I couldn't get through him. So, I picked Daisy up and told him I'd had enough and would be back for the boys in the morning. Then I ran with Daisy to the car.", she said as she looked down at her coffee.

"Ok, so, we get up in the morning and go get the boys.", Nanny told her.

"But, Mom, he chased me out the door and told me I'd never see them again.", she answered.

"Ohhhh, if he thinks he's keeping those boys, he's got another thing coming to him.", Nanny said with a chuckle.

As Nanny continued to console Mama I drifted off to sleep on the couch.

Chapter Four- (Matt)

After a while of sitting in the car listening to Mitch sing a broken song of, Twinkle, Twinkle, Little Star, for what felt like the hundredth time, Marc had fallen asleep and I was growing tired of waiting.

I twiddled my thumbs which started a game of thumb war with myself that eventually led to a world of army soldiers at war fighting in Japan.

"Come in Alpha One, I got him on my left.", I whispered into my invisible walkie talkie. I crouched down in the front seat of the car trying not to be seen by a man walking down the sidewalk. I held my invisible gun, aimed and ready to fire. My eyes were glued to him as he walked past the front of our car, "T-t-t-t-t, t-t!", I pretended to shoot. As he moved out of sight I continued, "T-t-t-t-t!".

When I could no longer see him I grabbed my walkie talkie again, pretending to put it to my mouth and removing my invisible helmet from my head. Excitedly, I shouted, "Alpha One, come in Alpha One, this is MM number one. I got him! Did you hear me? I got him!". I cheered for myself, clapping. I grabbed an imaginary cigar from the front pocket of my shirt and put it between my lips. Pretending to take a puff, I blew out the imaginary smoke and sat back, crossing my feet up on the dash and smiling at my imaginary accomplishment.

Just then, Dad came out of the office I'd watched him walk into, breaking my invisible world into a cloud that immediately drifted away. I quickly took my feet off the dash and sat back up in my seat.

He hurried out, opening the door and slid into his seat behind the wheel, smiling. He slapped me on the back of the head, "What have I told you about putting your feet on the dash?", he asked.

I put my head down and looked at the holes in the knees of my pants.

He shoved some papers he had walked out with into the glove compartment and then slid his hand over his hair to push it in place. Sitting straight up, he turned the car on and put it in reverse. As he turned to look behind him he whispered, "I've got her this time.".

As we began driving I was ready to see Mama. I just knew that's where we were headed next. Instead, we ended up at the hardware store.

Maybe this is the last stop before Nanny's, I thought.

Dad parked the car, "Come on.", he said as he got out.

He opened the backdoor, pulled out Mitch and nudged Marc awake, "Marcus, come on boy.", he said as he held Mitch in his arms.

I got out of the car and ran around to his side.

As Marc rubbed his eyes, waking up, he slowly began to crawl out of the car, "Are we getting Mommy?", he asked.

Dad leaned in still holding Mitch and grabbed Marc by the shirt directing him out of the car, "I don't have all day, boy. Now, quit asking questions and come on!", he told him.

I walked by Dad's side as he carried Mitch and held Marc's hand all the way into the store.

Being the oldest, I knew not to ask questions when Dad was on a mission so I kept my mouth shut the whole time.

Marc, on the other hand, still hadn't figured out when to shut up.

"Daddy?", he asked, "Why are we here? Are we getting Mommy?".

"Just come on.", Dad irritatedly answered, pulling on Marc's hand.

When we got inside, Dad put Mitch down to walk. The three of us followed Dad up to the first person we saw with a smock tied around his waist.

"Hey, sir, could you help me find the locks?", Dad asked the man.

The man nodded, "Right this way.". Then, the man led us down each aisle until we stood in front of rows of locks and doorknobs. Looking at the rows, I never realized how many different locks there were. Some had chains, some had hooks, some had little chambers, some were shiny and some were dull.

"Thank you, this is it.", Dad told the man.

"Yes, sir, and if you need anything else just let me know.", the man told him.

Dad looked at him, smiled and said with a chuckle, "Maybe some duct tape, rope and a sledge hammer.".

The man chuckled back nervously as Dad added, "I'm just fooling with you. Just having some lady problems, if you know what I mean.".

The man nodded, this time chuckling a little less nervously and said as he walked away, "Oh, boy, do I know about that!".

When the man was finally off down the next aisle, Dad began searching through the locks. Picking up one after another saying something like, "No, too big.", or "Too thin.".

Marc walked up the aisle looking at the locks. He reached in to touch one and then another, until he found one that slid. He picked it up and began sliding the lock back and forth. Dad looked over to see Marc playing with the lock and slapped it out of his hands, "Boy!", Dad said sternly. The lock fell out of Marc's hands and onto the floor.

"Pick it up!", Dad said as he grabbed Marc by the collar of his shirt.

Marc reached down to pick up the lock and placed it back on the shelf. As Marc backed away from the shelf, Dad reached down and swatted him on his butt, "Not another damn thing, Marcus. Don't touch another damn thing.", he said to him as he grabbed Marc's hand.

Holding two locks he had found, Dad nodded his head at Mitch and I to follow him, "Come on. I've got what I need.".

I grabbed Mitch's hand and we followed Dad down the aisle to check out.

As we drove away from the hardware store and down the street, my mind wandered back to Mama. Maybe now we'd go get her and Daisy.

Dad began singing as he drove, "When you say that I should phone...then I do and there's nobody home...la la la la...I've had it.", he sang and hummed, "When you say that you love me honey...hmmm, hmm, hmmm...when you really need my money...la la la la...hmmm, hmm...I've had it, oh yeah, I've had it.". He tapped the steering wheel as he drove and sang.

To my disappointment, we did not end up at Nanny's. Instead, we pulled into the driveway of our house.

It was a white, three bedroom bungalow that sat in a row of identical houses on the street. I had friends throughout the neighborhood that I played with outside but Jake was the best of them. We'd run up and down the street or ride our bikes.

There was a small baseball field a few blocks from our street that we'd go play ball at. It was my best way to escape. On the field, I didn't have to think or worry about anything but baseball. I'd never played on a real team before but always dreamed I would one day. Since Marc and Mitch weren't allowed to leave the yard, I rode my bike as often as I could to that field. The other boys in the neighborhood would join me and Jake there where we'd play for hours, hitting ball after ball and running through makeshift bases from some large stones we had found. I adored the legend, Babe Ruth. I tried my best to act like him as I pretended to stomp out a cigar, take my place to bat and then point my bat to the outfield, hoping to hit a homerun.

That day, when we got home from the hardware store, the four of us piled out of our 1955 blue Station Wagon. Dad got a small red toolbox out of the back. Carrying the toolbox, he went straight to the front door and began taking off the lock, "You boys run on. Go play.", he told us.

I didn't stop to question him as I ran to get my bike. When Dad said to go play, he meant he didn't want to be bothered.

Marc and Mitch had learned this too, although Marc always stopped to ask just before running off, "Why Daddy? What are you working on?".

Then Dad would grumble something and then wave his hand at him, "What did I tell you to do, boy?", he'd answer in irritation.

While Marc and Mitch went to play in our backyard I rode my bike three houses down to Jake's house.

I wondered about Mama and Daisy all the way there. Something about her leaving this time felt very different. It just wasn't like her to leave us boys behind this long and she'd never left us behind when she went to Nanny's after a fight.

Jake and I rode our bikes down to the field where I could finally take my mind off of it all for a little while. I was sure Mama would be back in time to make supper.

Chapter Five- (Daisy)

The next morning, Nanny was up early while Mama was still next to me on the couch where she had fallen asleep.

As I opened my eyes I could feel Mama breathing heavily next to me. Her arm was around me with her hand tucked under my back with my head resting on her chest. As I awoke, I pushed her arm just enough to wiggle out from underneath and crawl off the couch. I kissed her on the cheek as she rolled over still sleeping then I went to find Nanny who was in the kitchen humming and cooking.

As I walked in she turned to see me, "Well, there you are, little one.", she smiled. She put down the spatula that she had been holding and walked towards me to pick me up.

Kissing me on the head and giving me a gentle squeeze, she then placed me in a chair at the table.

"I've got pancakes coming right up.", she said to me as she walked back to the griddle on the stove.

"Did you sleep ok?", she asked me as I rubbed my tired eyes. I nodded my head and looked around the room.

"Where's my Bubbas?", I asked her.

"Well, they're still with your Daddy, sugar, but we'll go and get them as soon as we're finished eating breakfast.", she answered.

"Good morning.", I heard Mama say behind me as she entered the kitchen. Her nose was no longer bloody but her eye had a small bruise underneath. She scratched her head and spoke in a groggy voice, "Is there any coffee?", she asked.

Nanny flipped two pancakes onto a plate, set it in front of me and then grabbed a coffee cup out of the cabinet to hand to Mama.

As Mama poured herself some coffee she began, "Well, I guess I've got some cleaning up to do today.".

Nanny was flipping another pancake on the griddle when she turned around, "What are you cleaning up?", she asked.

Mama took a sip of her coffee and touched her bruised eye, "The mess I made yesterday. ", she answered.

"I'm not sure you made any kind of mess, honey.", Nanny replied as she flipped two more pancakes onto a plate and set it in front of Mama.

"Seems to me someone else has a mess of their own to clean up.", she added.

"Well, I did have another man's...", Mama stopped mid sentence and looked over at me as I dipped a piece of pancake into the syrup on my plate.

Nanny flipped two more pancakes onto a plate, turned the griddle off and sat down to join us.

As she reached for the syrup she asked, "What? A phone number? A plumber's phone number?".

She looked at Mama as she took a bite and stared directly into her eyes.

Mama looked down at her plate of pancakes, "Well.", was all she had to say.

"Look here, Mabel, we're going to enjoy our breakfast. Then, we'll get dressed and go to your house.", Nanny devised a plan as she took another bite, "When we get there you'll pack a few things for you and the kids. I'll have a few words with Mr. Mike and then we'll come back here.", sticking her fork into another piece of pancake, "With ALL of the kids.", she said.

Mama didn't reply as she took a couple of bites and then pushed her plate away. She stood up from the table and gently rubbed the top of my head as she took her unfinished plate to the sink.

"I've got to use the restroom.", she said as she left the kitchen.

"Listen, Daisy.", Nanny looked at me, "There isn't a man in the world worth being a punching bag for.", she said as she continued to eat. I nodded my head as I scooped another piece of pancake into my mouth.

After breakfast, Nanny got ready to go as Mama began cleaning up and folding the blanket we had slept under the night before.

Mama washed my face with a rag and combed my hair.

"Ready?", Nanny asked as she came out with her hair in perfect little curls and wearing red lipstick.

Mama nodded and grabbed me by the hand as we left to go get my brothers.

In the car, Mama held me in her lap in the front seat. We rode in Nanny's Buick, as she drove, reminding Mama of the plan.

"I'll be right there with you, Mabel. You just go in there and get some things packed and I'll handle the devil.", she said seriously.

Mama stared out the window and stroked my hair as we drove, "But what if...", she began as Nanny interrupted, "No ma'am, there isn't going to be any ifs.", Nanny said sternly.

I could feel Mama's hand run through my hair a little slower and grab the strands a little tighter.

As we turned onto our street, she began breathing heavier, gently squeezing me around the middle.

We pulled up behind Daddy's car. Nanny parked, took a deep breath and said, "Here we go.".

Mama rolled down the window, kissed the top of my head and whispered in my ear, "You stay right here, Daisy. You hear me?".

I sat up on my knees to get a better view out the window.

Nanny got out of the car and walked up to the house ready to take care of business as Mama followed.

When they got to the door, Mama jiggled the handle but it was locked, "Its locked?", she asked out loud as she dug through the purse that was hanging on her shoulder and pulled out her keys. Nanny was pacing around on the front porch, looking up and down the street as she lit a cigarette.

Mama put the key into the doorknob only to find it wouldn't unlock. She looked at Nanny confused and tried the key again and then again.

Unsuccessful, Mama began to look panicked. Holding the keys in her hand she looked back down at them and then held them up, pushing through each of the three keys on the keyring.

"I know that's the right one. It has to be.", she said. Nanny took the keys from Mama and tried each of the keys herself only to find it still wouldn't unlock.

Taking one more puff of her cigarette, Nanny threw it down on the porch and stomped it out.

Mama stepped off of the porch and stood on the sidewalk as Nanny began knocking on the door, "Mike?", she called out, "Mike, open the door.", she demanded.

She continued knocking, harder now as Mama began walking around in circles.

"Mike, I'll get the police involved if I need to.", Nanny hollered through the door.

Just then the door cracked open just enough for Daddy to poke through, squeeze outside and shut it behind him. He stood in front of Nanny, pushing his hair over with his hand, he crossed his arms and smirked at Nanny.

"Well, hello, Peggy.", he spoke softly, " What brings you here?".

"My grandsons.", Nanny spoke quietly as she stood nearly nose to nose with Daddy.

"We don't want any trouble, Mike, we just want the boys and we'll be out.", Nanny added.

Daddy pulled a piece of paper out of his shirt pocket, unfolded it and held it in front of Nanny.

"Says here, Peggy, I don't have to let you take my boys anywhere.", he said as he held the paper in front of her face.

Nanny snatched the paper and began reading it to herself.

She wadded it into a ball and threw it at Daddy.

As it fell at his feet he bent down picking the ball of paper up and said, with a chuckle, "What are you going to do now, woman?". He stepped back into the house, shutting the door as Nanny tried pushing the door open behind him without success.

"This isn't the end, Mike! We're getting those boys!", she slapped her hand on the door, "You hear me?", she yelled.

She turned to walk back to the car grabbing Mama on her way. As they got back in the car, Mama began crying, "What did it say? The paper?", Mama asked Nanny.

Nanny got in, "Hop in the back, Daisy.", she told me.

I climbed over the seat to the back, crawling close to the window to look out.

"Well, it said he's decided to go to war with us.", Nanny said as she glared over the steering wheel and backed out without looking behind her.

"War?", Mama whispered.

"Yes, baby, war. Put your gear on, this is fixing to be a battle we're going to have to fight hard to win.", Nanny answered.

War?, I thought. My little mind imagined soldiers hiding down behind bunkers with helmets and big guns. I became worried as the soldiers turned into Nanny and Mama getting blown to pieces by a grenade thrown by Daddy from the other side of the bunker.

We drove into town and stopped at an office building with lots of windows.

"Come on, Mabel, let's go set things straight.", Nanny puffed her hair in the rearview mirror and then straightened the collar on her dress.

Mama didn't even look at herself as she got out of the car. I followed Mama, holding her hand as Nanny marched in front of us straight inside the building.

As she opened the glass door a little bell rang as it hit the inside of the door. We entered into some kind of smokey office with a waiting room and a lady behind a counter who was typing on a typewriter. Nanny went up to the counter while Mama took me to sit with her in a chair to wait.

"Hello, what can I do for you?", the lady behind the counter spoke. She had long blonde hair, pulled back into a bun and wore dark rimmed glasses that she nudged back up into place on her nose.

"Hi, my name is Peggy Culhane and this is my daughter, Mabel Mair.", Nanny motioned to where Mama and I were sitting, "We need to speak with Mr. Thompson, please.".

The lady looked at a notebook that was laid open in front of her on her desk. She ran her finger across the page, then looked up at Nanny, "I'm sorry, I don't have, did you say Culhane? I don't see you on the schedule, ma'am.", she told Nanny.

"Oh, no, we don't have an appointment. We've had something come up that involves Mr. Thompson that we'd like to speak with him about.", Nanny smiled a sly smile as she clenched her purse in her hands.

"Oh, well, in that case, I'll let him know you're here, but he may not be able to see you today.", the lady answered.

Nanny reached into a dish that sat on the counter and grabbed a mint. She unwrapped it slowly and then held the mint between her fingers as she spoke, "Ma'am, make sure to let him know, we've got all day and we aren't going anywhere until we speak to him.", Nanny popped the mint into her mouth, smiled and turned around to come join us to wait.

As Nanny sat down beside Mama and I, the lady got up from behind the desk and opened a door leading out of the waiting area. She poked her head inside and spoke quietly to someone behind the door, "Mr. Thompson?".

We heard a deep, gruff voice from behind the door answer with an impatient huff, "What is it Pearl?".

"Mr. Thompson, there's a Peggy Culhane here to see you. Seems important.", the lady told the man behind the door.

With a long sigh the man said, "Send her in, but tell her I don't have much time.".

The lady nodded and left the door slightly open behind her as she came back into the waiting area.

"Mr. Thompson said he can see you now, but he has an appointment coming in so he won't be able to speak with you long.", the lady said to Nanny.

Nanny jumped up out of the chair she was sitting in, patting Mama on the back as she stood. Mama grabbed me by the hand as we followed Nanny who had pushed past the lady and was already pushing open the door to the office. She knocked lightly as she barged in letting Mama and I in behind her.

There was a very round-faced man with a large round belly wearing a pin striped, button up shirt and suspenders that looked like they might pop off of his pants at any moment. He was holding a cigar between his fingers as he pushed some papers to the side of his desk. He had sweat rolling down his face from the top of his nearly bald head. I couldn't believe how shiny his head was so I stared intently at it as the adults in the room began to speak.

"Hello, Mr. Thompson.", Nanny said in a low, serious voice, her eyes in a squint and eyebrows down.

"Hello, Peggy, how have you been?", he said as if he knew her.

"Well, I've been better. Of course, I'm sure you know what brings me in today.", Nanny answered.

The man nodded and sat back in his chair as he dropped some ashes from his cigar into the ashtray on his desk and then took a puff. He blew the smoke out as Nanny reached into her purse and pulled out her cigarettes.

"Mind if I join you?", before he could answer, she lit the cigarette dangling from her mouth.

She inhaled the smoke from the cigarette deeply and blew it out above her head then crossed her legs and pulled the ashtray closer towards her.

"Let's not dilly dally here, Mr. Thompson, let's get straight to business. Seeing you have an appointment soon and everything.", Nanny stared with cutting eyes at the man.

He dabbed out his cigar into the ashtray and then folded his fingers together, resting them on his belly, "Listen, Peggy, the man came in and...", Nanny interrupted, "You promised me the last time a man screwed me over with your help that you'd be on my side next time.".

"Well, that changed when he brought money to the table.", the man said as he waved his hands in front of him.

Nanny rolled her eyes, "Of course, he brought money. How much?", she asked.

"I'm not obliged to say.", the man sat up, "What I can say is this, he's got a good argument. ", he lowered his eyes and then glanced over at Mama and I who were sitting together in a chair next to Nanny.

Nanny turned to look at Mama as if she knew what he was talking about and then back to the man.

"So, are you obliged to tell me his argument?", Nanny put her cigarette out in the ashtray and leaned close to the man with her elbows on the desk, staring into his eyes.

He shrugged his shoulders, "He came in, said he needed to get custody of his boys. Said his wife was a...", pausing, he glanced again at Mama and I, cleared his throat as he changed his mind on what he was about to say, "...said she'd been talking to another man and that she'd ran off.".

Nanny looked over at Mama who was looking down at the floor, with me still in her lap.

"Did he tell you why she ran off?", Nanny reached over and put her hand under Mama's chin, pushing her face up to show him her black eye.

SEARCHING FOR HER BOYS: A SEARCH FOR HOPE   33

The man cleared his throat, "He said he did have a squabble with her but that he was right to be angry.", he looked away from Mama, "He wanted to teach her a lesson.".

Nanny, sitting straight up now, "So, you're telling me that Mike Mair waltzed in here and said he hit his wife and now he's taking her boys to teach her a lesson for talking to another man? I don't know if he made it clear to you, but did he tell you the man she was talking to was the plumber?", Nanny slapped her hand on the desk, "I don't know why she needs a lesson for calling another man to come fix the sink. Sounds like he needs a lesson on how to take care of things around the house and maybe not hitting ladies.".

The man waved his hand in the air at Nanny, "He never mentioned any hitting going on and he said she ran off and left them.", the man said as he shrugged his shoulders again, "He even pointed to the boys sitting in the car waiting on him.".

Nanny pushed the ashtray on the man's desk back towards him, "So, you just said you could file a paper for that when you saw green on the table, is that what I understand?", Nanny asked in disbelief.

As he sat up in his chair the man answered, "Well, Peggy, the man had the boys, the mother was nowhere in sight and yes he had money so...", Nanny interrupted the man again,

"So, what about the girl? He forgot he had a daughter?".

The man scratched his bald head and said in a hushed voice, "He says he isn't the father of the girl.", he shrugged one more time. "I'm sorry, Peggy, but it'll be filed in the morning and his story makes more sense.".

Nanny stood up, "Makes more sense? I'll tell you what makes more sense, you burning in hell with him for supporting a wife beater!", she threw her purse over her shoulder, "Come on, Mabel, we don't need to waste any more time with this pathetic sack of...", pausing as she looked down at me, "manure.".

Mama grabbed my hand as we followed Nanny out of the office and back to the car.

As Nanny began to drive, she mumbled curse words in between other words that I didn't recognize.

Mama held me in her lap and finally spoke, "He's going to take my boys?", she asked in a whisper.

Nanny didn't respond.

"He's going to take my boys?", Mama repeated a little louder.

With no response from Nanny who was clutching the steering wheel with white knuckles, Mama repeated her question louder this time, "He's going to take my boys?", she wailed as she wrapped her arms tightly around me, crying into the back of my head.

The plan to go get my brothers had somehow turned into a tragedy that, little did I or even Mama know at the time, was only just beginning.

Chapter Six- (Matt)

Jake and I got to the open field and began throwing a baseball back and forth to each other.

I tried hard not to worry about Mama as I threw the ball harder with each pass. I thought about Dad yelling last night and calling Mama names and hearing Daisy crying. I thought about watching Dad through the window chasing Mama out the door and her bleeding. The more I thought, the madder I got. I wasn't really sure what exactly I was mad about, but I could feel it rising in my body as I threw the ball, now seeing Jake as some sort of target for my anger.

"Owww!", Jake hollered as the ball hit his shoulder. He grabbed his arm,"What's your problem?", he asked with hurt in his voice.

As he rubbed his shoulder, I walked closer to him and stood in front of him, "I'm sorry, I'm really sorry.", I said, "I didn't know you weren't ready.", making it seem as though it was more of an accident than it really was. I needed someone to take my frustration out on and it just so happened to be Jake.

"I was ready! You just threw it right at me!", he whined.

"Oh, come on, it was an accident.", I patted him on the shoulder and then ran back to my place on the field, "Come on, I'll be easier.", holding my mitt up ready to catch.

Jake rubbed his shoulder and then shook his arm as if to shake away the pain. He pulled his arm back and threw the ball as hard as he could, hurling it right into my hip. I fell to the ground, curling up and holding my hip, "Ahhhh!", I cried out, "Okay, Okay, I said I was sorry, damn it!", I only cursed when my parents weren't around. I didn't know what would happen to me if they ever heard me, at least if Dad heard anyway.

Jake ran to my side, bent over and said, "paybacks", as he reached out his hand to help me sit up. Looking up at him I nodded through my moaning,"paybacks", I answered.

That was our way of making everything right between us again.

"Jake...", I started as I sat up, "I'm worried about my Mama.", I told him as he sat down on the ground next to me. He pulled out a package of sunflower seeds from his pocket and offered me some. I held my hands out for him to pour a small pile into my palms.

"Why are you worried about your Mama?", Jake asked.

He was a little shorter than me and had much darker hair than my almost white, blonde color. He had chubby cheeks with a very deep dimple in his chin. Mama loved to squeeze his chin when he'd come ask for me to play, "Of course, sweetie, I'll go get him.", she'd say.

I was the only blonde kid on our street, even in my family. I was as Nanny would say, "long and lanky". I was going through a growth spurt at the time and seemed to be busting out of all of my clothes. I felt like the Incredible Hulk with the way my pants were starting to fit. Eight years old and nearly taller than some of the ten year olds on our street. I had been enjoying summer with my friends, but nights like last night made me long for school to start. At school, I could think about other things than home, even if school was the one thing I disliked most. I wasn't very good at it, all the writing and reading. One of my teachers once made me stand up in front of the class to read something I had written because she said it was an example of a failing grade. I remember everyone in class snickering as I read quietly, barely able to even read my own writing. I don't remember what it said but I do remember how I felt in that moment, small, which was how I felt at home when Dad was there. Times like that made me want to run. If only I could just run away and be free from it all is what I always thought.

Jake and I sat there, chewing on sunflower seeds, "I don't know.", I answered, "She was pretty upset when she left last night and so was my old man.".

Jake spit out the shell of a sunflower seed,"Oh, you know how they do. She always comes back after they fight.", he said as he crunched on the seeds in his mouth.

"Yeah, but something feels different this time. She never leaves without us.", I spit a shell as far as I could, "And my old man went to some office today and then got new locks for the doors.".

I only called my dad an old man when I was talking with friends. I would never call him that to his face.

"He got new locks?", Jake spit out another shell, this time trying to make it land further than mine.

"Yeah, he's putting them on right now.", I said, spitting another shell even further than the one Jake had just spit out.

Just then, we saw Nanny's car drive past the field from a distance, headed straight down our street.

"See, there she is, she's coming back.", Jake said with encouragement.

I stood up, trying to see Nanny's car as it blended in with the trees that surrounded the field.

My heart began pounding with excitement as I spit the last shell of a seed on the ground and picked up my mitt.

"Let's go!", I hollered at Jake as I ran to get on my bike. Jake ran behind me and picked up his bike that was laying beside mine. As we both began walking alongside our bikes it hit me, they're in Nanny's car, not Mama's.

I stopped for a moment and put my hand up to motion for Jake to stop too.

"What is it?", he asked.

"They're in my Nanny's car.", I answered.

"So?", Jake shrugged.

"So, they're not in my Mama's. Where's her car?", I looked back at Jake.

My Dad was a car guy and at the time we had more cars than anyone on our street.

Most everyone could only afford one, but my Dad was somehow able to have two, one for him and one for Mama. Hers was an old beat up Sedan he had paid in cash for at some old lot after one of their fights. He told her she could have it if she came back.

We quickly got on our bikes and began riding to the end of our street. We hid behind some bushes in a neighbor's yard that blocked us from being seen from my house.

I watched as Nanny pounded on the door. I could see Mama walking in circles behind her and Daisy in the front seat of Nanny's car .

Nanny paced around on the front porch when Dad came out. I couldn't hear what they were saying but Nanny looked mad as Dad stood in front of the door with his arms crossed, no expression on his face.

I could just barely see Marc and Mitch playing with some old metal toy trucks just inside the chain link fence that blocked the backyard. They continued playing, seeming unbothered by what I was watching.

Nanny poked Dad in the shoulder as he stepped back still with his arms crossed.

"This isn't the end, Mike Mair!", I heard her yell as she walked back to her car with Mama following behind. As she opened the car door, "You hear me, you asshole? You hear me?", she looked at him as if waiting for an answer from him.

"This isn't the end!", she yelled as she finally got inside the car and slammed the door.

I watched as Nanny pulled out of the driveway and sped away with Mama and Daisy. Dad, finally showing emotion with a smile, waved goodbye and then turned around. He went back inside the house, shutting the door behind him.

I turned to look at Jake,

"I wonder what that was all about?", he said to me as I searched in my mind for some kind of answer.

We got on our bikes and rode closer.

"I better go see what's going on.", I said to him as we got to his house.

"Okay, see you later.", he said as he laid his bike down in his front yard.

"I bet she's home by supper.", he added, "Don't worry too much about it, man.", he said before turning to go inside his house.

I rode to my house and laid my bike down.

As I stepped up onto the porch I took a deep breath before grabbing the doorknob to go inside. As I exhaled, I turned the knob only to find it wouldn't turn. It was locked. Confused as to why it was locked since we never locked the door, not even when we were gone for the day, I gently knocked.

I heard it unlock and Dad appeared as he cracked the door open saying, "You come back for more?".

Looking straight ahead through the opening, he realized it wasn't Nanny and looked down to see me standing there.

He opened the door and motioned for me to come in as he looked up and down our street.

I went in and plopped on the couch.

"When's Mama coming back?", I asked.

"Well, boy, I don't think she is. Not tonight at least.", he walked into the kitchen and opened up the refrigerator.

He grabbed a beer, opened it and took a big long drink until it was almost empty. He looked over at me as he pushed his hair with his hand to the side.

I wasn't really sure what to say next and I sure didn't want to make him angry with me next so I chose my words very carefully, "So, then, what's for supper?", I decided was the best thing to say.

Without answering, he took the last drink from his beer bottle and threw it in the trash.

He never answered as he went to the back door to holler for Marc and Mitch to come inside.

They whined as they came in, "But Dad-dy, we weren't finished.", Marc said as he came in with Mitch tripping over the steps of our back porch.

They came in and Marc plopped onto the couch next to me. Mitch climbed up behind him. The three of us sat there in silence as we watched Dad pace around in the kitchen.

"Where's Mommy?", Mitch asked me.

I put my finger to my lips to signal for him to be quiet and shook my head.

Again he asked, "Where's Mommy?".

Then, Marc joined in with the same question, "Yeah, where's Mama?".

Dad sat down in his big chair beside the couch, "Your mother isn't coming home tonight.", he answered.

"Why, Daddy?", Marc asked, "Why not?".

"She's off at your Nanny's.", he answered. "Now, you've got your answer, so no more questions about it.".

Mitch rolled down off of the couch and went to grab the Lincoln logs that were still on the floor. Marc and I watched as Mitch began building, unaware that he should be concerned about why Mama was at Nanny's without us and also wasn't coming back before supper.

Marc watched for a while as he sat there beside me. Dad got up and went to the kitchen to begin figuring out what would suffice us for supper.

Marc looked over at me and whispered, "Is Mama coming home tomorrow?".

I sat there, not knowing for sure the answer but knowing he needed one, "Yeah, I bet she'll be back tomorrow.", was all I could think to say.

"What about Daisy?", he then asked.

"Yeah, her too, they'll be back tomorrow.", I said.

Marc leaned over next to my side, resting his head on my shoulder, "I really miss them.", he whispered.

I put my arm around him as we continued watching Mitch play on the floor, "Me too, brother, me too.".

Chapter Seven- (Daisy)

As we drove away from the office, Mama became a blubbering mess which only fueled Nanny's anger.

She drove faster as Mama continued to cry into the back of my head, squeezing me tighter. The only thing I could do was hold tight to her arms, "Mama, it ok, Mama,", I tried to reassure her with my four year old voice.

Nanny began talking out loud to herself, "I've had enough. He thinks I'm crazy, well, he hasn't seen crazy yet.", she rattled off, "This isn't the end."

She drove until she got to our street and once again pulled into our driveway. This time she didn't wait for Mama to get out.

"Wait here.", she said as she slammed the car door behind her.

She walked up to the door of our house and began pounding, "Mike!", she hollered, "Mike Mair, you come out here and face me like a man."

Soon, Daddy appeared as he opened the door and closed it behind him. Crossing his arms he said nothing.

"How dare you!", Nanny began, "You are nothing but a slimy, asshole."

He smirked as Nanny threw insults at him, never moving from his position on the porch.

"You hit my baby girl! You wife beater!", she continued, "And if you think you're getting away with that, you have another thing coming."

His responding smirk only seemed to fire Nanny up more.

"You won't take those babies from her.", she said as she walked away, "I'll see to it!", she added as she got back in the car.

I watched, as we drove away, Daddy walked back inside seeming unphased by Nanny.

I could see Marc and Mitch playing out back through the chain link fence and I wondered when I'd play with them again.

As we drove down our street, Mama continued crying, saying, "He's taking my boys.", over and over.

The bushes outside of a house down the street stuck out to me as we drove by, there were two bikes hiding behind them with two faces poking out. As we passed them, I realized those faces were Matt and his friend, Jake. I pulled myself out from underneath Mama's arms and sat straight up to get a better look out of the window. I stared at them as we turned off of our street and drove away. Reaching as far as I could to see out of the window, they faded out of my view.

When we returned to Nanny's house, Mama could barely follow her inside. I'd never seen her so weak. It was as if her legs were made of jello, wobbling as she walked.

She fell onto the couch and hugged a pillow that laid beside her. I wasn't really sure what to do so I decided to go play with the toys Nanny had for us in a big old wooden toy chest in her guest room. There, I could pretend nothing happened and go into an imaginary world where everything was safe.

After a few days of being at Nanny's though, it started to feel like we may never go home. I was starting to miss my brothers and playing by myself was becoming lonely. The toys in the toy chest were starting to lose their wonder.

Nanny had gone through all of her hiding spots in the house to find the money she'd been stashing. Together, her and Mama counted it all out on the kitchen table, "Eight hundred fifty two.", Nanny said as she placed the last bill in the pile, "I'd have more if it wasn't for that last asshole.", she wrinkled her eyebrows.

"Now what?", Mama asked.

"Well, now, we go find someone to help get our boys back.", she told Mama,"The paper only said that as long as you're not there, the boys stay with him.".

"So what are we going to do to get them back?", Mama asked as she picked up a straightened stack of bills on the table, "The only way I can see is for me and Daisy to go home."

"No, you aren't going back there.", Nanny said sternly, "Why? So he can black your other eye? I mean, the sink probably still needs to be fixed and that isn't worth calling Pete the plumber for."

Mama shrugged, "You're right, but I just don't see any other way.", Mama put her elbows on the table and rested her face in her hand, "I either go back and be with my boys or I stay here and...", her words trailed off as she looked away.

"No, there's got to be another way.", Nanny answered, "We're not done fighting yet. I know someone we can take this money to that can maybe help us."

I was sitting at the coffee table in front of the couch, just outside of the kitchen listening in as I colored a picture in a farm coloring book. Nanny had gotten it for me as a special treat for being such a good girl at the supermarket.

"You have been such a wonderful helper, baby girl.", she smiled at me as she scanned a magazine rack that was sitting at the checkout counter looking for her favorite, Glamour.

Nanny loved reading the beauty tips and dating advice columns.

Just then there was a knock at the door.

Nanny and Mama looked at each other, "Expecting anyone?", Nanny asked as Mama shook her head and shrugged her shoulders.

Nanny got up and scooped the money off the table, "Be right there!", she hollered at the door.

She quickly opened the kitchen cabinet to find a canning jar and stuffed the money inside. She went to the door, unlocking each lock and cracking it open to peek outside. I couldn't see who was there but I heard a man's voice, "Hello, Peggy.", the deep manly voice said.

"Oh, hello, sherriff.", Nanny answered, "Is everything alright?".

"Oh, yes ma'am, everything's fine. Mabel doesn't happen to be here does she?", the voice asked.

When Mama heard her name she got up from the kitchen table and walked towards the door.

"Well, yes sir, she's here. Can I ask what's going on?", Nanny answered as she opened the door a little more. Mama walked up behind Nanny and stood behind her at the door.

"Mabel Mair, you've been served.", the voice said as he handed Mama a big brown envelope. Mama and Nanny looked down at the envelope and then at each other. Mama reluctantly took the envelope and nodded her head. Then, the voice moved away from the door and said, "Have a nice day ladies.".

Nanny closed the door, turning to look at Mama who was now standing frozen with the envelope in her hands.

Nanny put her hands on Mama's shoulders and turned her towards the kitchen, " Well, let's see what this is about. ", she said as she guided Mama back to the kitchen table.

They sat down at the table as I continued coloring.

Mama slowly opened up the envelope and pulled out a stack of papers. She flipped through each page, reading them in silence. Then, she shoved them in front of Nanny and put her face in her hands as she began to cry.

Nanny grabbed the papers and began to read pieces of them out loud, "In the matter of the marriage of Michael Mair and Mabel Mair...divorce...in the matter of Matthew Mair, Marcus Mair and Mitchell Mair...abandoned...full custody.", her mouth dropped open and she stopped reading as she put the papers down on the table. Not knowing what to say she looked over at me.

Smiling at her I asked, "Okay, Nanny?".

She smiled back at me but didn't answer.

The woman who seemed to have an answer for everything seemed, for the first time, stumped.

I wasn't sure what it meant to be served but it didn't seem like anything good.

Chapter Eight- (Matt)

A few nights went by without Mama and I had become Dad's full time helper. It was different from helping Mama with the daily chores which I didn't mind doing. We did the dishes together every night. She'd wash each one and then hand them to me to dry with a towel. We'd talk about school and my friends as we worked together. I also helped bring clothes in from the line out back. Mama and I would each carry a basket to hold the clothes we plucked down. Every once in a while, she would look back at my brothers and Daisy as they played and smile. We'd carry the baskets in, heaping with clothes and then she'd tell me I'd done a good job and allow me to go play.

Now, I was doing the chores alone.

Mama's soft voice had been replaced with Dad's booming voice, "Matthew!", Dad would holler and I'd answer, "Yes, sir?".

"Get your brothers some clothes.", "Go wash them dishes.", "Get this mess cleaned up." or "Take them boys outside.", he'd grumble.

I knew not to talk back to Dad, but I was getting tired of doing all of Mama's jobs around the house and so, less eager to help out, I slowly began to shrug my shoulders as I would walk away after hearing my orders. I don't think I realized, until she was gone, just how much she did.

I wondered where she was and why she hadn't come back yet.

It wasn't like her, staying gone like this and without us boys. I missed Daisy too. She was my little buddy. I loved how she looked at me when I'd help her do things or play with her. She looked a lot like Mitch with dark, wavy hair and deep brown eyes. Her cheeks were chubby and she was beginning to grow the "Mair point" in her nose, as our family called it.

Daisy was, for the most part, quiet. She was a watcher. Always watching us boys or Mama and then trying to mimic us.

One time, after watching Mama set the table every night, Daisy had gathered plates and silverware from the kitchen while Mama was changing out clothes on the line in our backyard. When Mama came back in with a basket of clothes, we heard Daisy from her room, "Okay, ev-ee-body, time to eat!". She came out wearing one of her polka-dotted dresses folded and wrapped around her waist, as if it were an apron, tucked into her underpants.

"It getting cold.", she added with her chubby, little, toothy smile.

Mama sat the basket down, wiped her hands on her dress, looked over at me with a wink and asked, "Ohhh, what did you make us this time, Daisy?".

"Skettie.", Daisy answered as she went back to the "table" she had set in her bedroom. Mama and I followed, "Come on boys! Daisy made supper tonight!", Mama said as we went to the bedroom.

Mama wasn't expecting to see her good plates and silverware laid out on a blanket in the middle of Daisy's bedroom floor. She stopped as soon as she saw what Daisy had done and for a moment I thought she might get upset. Instead, she took a deep breath and went inside, sitting down on the floor at the "table" Daisy had prepared for us. Marc and Mitch came in right behind us. We all enjoyed Daisy's "skettie", pretending to scoop it onto our forks and into our mouths. Each of us made smacking noises while we pretended to eat. Afterwards, Mama had each of us take our plates and silverware back to the kitchen where Mama quietly put them away later.

After that, the next time we visited Nanny, there was a plastic set of toy dishes waiting for Daisy.

"Now you can use your very own plates to make us something to eat!", Mama told her excitedly.

Daisy didn't just watch Mama, she also watched me play and would often join me running around the yard shooting bad guys with my little plastic police gun.

As Officer Mair, I would duck behind a tree for cover, ready to shoot the "robber" who had just come out of our house. Just as I would spot the imaginary man running out of our back door, I'd aim and fire, "Pow, pow, p-p-p-pow!", shooting him and making him fall to the ground.

"Pow, pow!", Daisy repeated while I ran to arrest the man in our imaginary world.

I'd grab the plastic handcuffs that hung from my belt loop as Daisy would run up next to me to help, "Got him!", she'd say as she'd pretend to hold him down while I cuffed him.

Now, with Marc and Mitch who mostly played on their own with their cars and trucks, I was left to entertain myself, usually choosing to read a comic book.

Dad wasn't a cooker so we ate peanut butter sandwiches without Mama and I was getting tired of them right along with my brothers.

"Peanut butter? Again?", Marc complained as we sat at the table to eat.

While Marc began to poke a hole into the bread with his finger, Dad slapped the back of Marc's head, "You'll eat it, boy, or you'll eat nothing.", he told him.

Marc rubbed the back of his head and stuck out his bottom lip, crossing his arms and slouching back in his chair, he mumbled, "I want Mommy.".

Dad slapped the table in front of Marc causing us all to jump right along with everything that was on the table.

"Go.", Dad said low and deep, looking straight into Marc's eyes.

Mitch and I watched as Marc pushed himself away from the table to stand up and then ran to the bedroom crying.

Dad turned back to the table glaring at me and then Mitch as we dared not to speak, "Well?", he said as he picked up his sandwich, "Are you going to join him or are you going to eat?".

He took a bite of his sandwich as he waited for us to answer.

We each picked up our sandwiches and began nibbling at them, silently glancing at each other.

Supper had never been a very relaxed event when Dad was at the table, but without Mama there, it was nearly unbearable. She was no longer there to soften his verbal blows with a soft look or follow up his orders with something like, "It's okay, honey, you just have to do what you're told.".

Eventually, some time passed and we started back to school. I was in third grade and, for the first time, without Mama walking beside me all the way there. Instead, I was in charge of getting my brothers there.

As we would begin to leave, Dad would reach into his pocket for nickels to give to us for milk. He would pat us each on the head as we walked out the door. From there we'd part ways, with him heading to work and us down the street to school.

I wasn't sure how long it had been since Mama had left with Daisy but at that point I'd decided I may never see them again. Marc and Mitch still asked about her, sometimes crying for her, especially at bedtime.

I'd lie in my bed and look through the window at the stars, wondering what she was doing and if she was thinking about us.

It slowly began to seem like Dad had forgotten about them altogether. He didn't talk about them and when we did, he rolled his eyes and breathed deeply. I noticed his drinking had slowed down almost to an end but, unfortunately, not his temper.

One evening, he was in the bathroom combing his hair, as always, slicked to the side. He was wearing navy blue slacks, a white button up shirt and a navy blue tie. As he sat the comb down on the sink he looked at himself in the mirror and slid down one stray hair with his fingers, straightened his collar and then hollered, "Matthew! Don't forget Aunt Becky's number is by the phone!".

Aunt Becky had been helping Dad out since Mama had been gone. She was his younger sister. Although she was just a teenager, she was very mature for her age. I liked when she came over because she took care of the things that Mama always did. It made me feel like she was there through her in some way.

Dad came into the living room and slid on his brown jacket, the one he only wore on special occasions, grabbed his keys and as he walked towards the front door he turned back to say, "You boys open the door for Aunt Becky. She should be here soon. Until then, no foolishness."

He opened the door and let in the cool night air as he left.

As soon as I heard his car start and then back out of the driveway I let out a sigh.

I sat quietly on the couch as Mitch crept down the hall out of the bedroom. He was wearing his favorite red pajamas, the ones Mama had bought him for Christmas last year. He rubbed his eyes as he crawled up onto the couch next to me.

"Where'd Daddy go?", he asked as stuck his thumb in his mouth. Dad hated it when Mitch sucked his thumb, always reaching over to slap his hand away from his mouth.

Mitch learned quickly only to suck his thumb when Dad wasn't around.

I put my arm around him and answered, "Out."

We sat there, the two of us in the quiet waiting for Aunt Becky. The light from the kitchen was the only one on, giving us just enough light to not be in complete darkness.

After a while of sitting, Mitch began to fall asleep. As he leaned closer to me, his thumb still in his mouth, he rested his head on my side and whispered, " I miss Mommy."

With that little whisper from Mitch something sparked inside of me. It was a feeling I'd never felt before and I wasn't sure what it was. It felt more fierce than anger as it rose from my chest into my throat. I wanted to cry. "Boys don't cry.", I heard Dad's voice say so I held it in.

How could she do this?, I thought, She just left us and doesn't even care about us anymore?.

As those thoughts raced through my mind it fueled the feeling I was having at the time for her. I'd never felt this kind of anger towards Mama.

As Mitch began breathing heavier in his sleep my heart pounded. I thought she loved us, I thought she'd never leave us like this.

Then there was a knock on the door and a familiar voice spoke through it, "Matthew?", I heard it say, "Matt, it's Aunt Becky.".

I gently slid out from under Mitch and got up to answer the door. Aunt Becky walked in and closed the door behind her, locking it. She turned to look at me smiling and saying, "Hey kid, what are you up to?".

I stood there, glaring at her, imagining she was Mama.

She walked into the kitchen, sat her purse on the kitchen table and grabbed a glass from the cabinet to fill with water from the sink.

I imagined Mama at the sink and thought about all the things I would say to her.

Aunt Becky took a long drink from the glass and then sat it down on the counter. She turned to walk into the living area where I was standing. As she got closer to me, I balled up my fists that were down by my sides.

"What's the matter, Matt? You ok, kid?", she asked as she knelt down in front of me, putting her hand on my shoulder. I shrugged her hand away and with my fist hit her in the shoulder as hard as I could.

"Ow!", she hollered and grabbed her shoulder, quickly standing up. Looking at me with confusion and hurt she asked, " Matthew, what'd you do that for?".

She rubbed her shoulder as I ran off down the hall, yelling behind me, "I hate you!".

I jumped onto my bed and buried my face into my pillow as I let out a cry in anger. I pounded my fists into the sides of my pillow and flopped around quickly onto my back crossing my arms in front of me. I'd never hit a woman before. Dad had hit Mama lots of times and I always felt bad for her but this, this felt good. It felt good to punch her and I wasn't sure why because I loved Aunt Becky.

I laid there staring out the window at the stars, crying angrily. Silent tears began slowly rolling down my cheeks. I quickly began wiping each one away in shame before they could hit my pillow.

In that moment, something changed in how I saw Mama. Maybe Dad was right all this time. She only cared about her and Daisy.

Realizing I may never see either of them again, I closed my eyes and decided that tomorrow when I woke up it would be time to no longer be a boy that yearned for his mother, it was time to be a man and somehow move on just like Dad had done.

Chapter Nine- (Daisy)

Mama and I stayed with Nanny for the next few weeks, which for me felt more like months.

Mama had mostly spent her time laying around either crying or sleeping and Nanny made each meal with the hope that Mama would eventually eat.

"Come on, Mabel, you have to eat something already.", she said as she shoved a plate of bacon and eggs in front of Mama.

Reluctantly, Mama picked up a piece of bacon and took a bite, chewing slowly.

"We're going to see a lawyer today. You're going to need to get dressed and go with me.", Nanny told her.

Mama put the piece of bacon back on her plate and looked up at Nanny, "Will I ever see them again?", she asked Nanny who was now sitting across from her at the table.

"Of course you will, honey.", Nanny assured, "He can't keep them from their mother forever.".

Mama ate a couple of bites of her eggs and then slowly got up from the table. She walked with defeat down the hall to get ready.

Nanny looked over at me and pushed a strand of hair out of my face. I looked up at her and smiled with cheeks full of scrambled eggs.

"Let's hope this lady lawyer can help us.", Nanny said to me, "She's all we've got.".

Eventually, the three of us were ready to go. Mama had a light pink dress that Nanny had bought for her along with a strand of pearls around her neck and a pair of Nanny's pink heels. I hadn't seen Mama look like herself since the day we'd come back without the boys. Her dark hair was neatly curled around her face where the bruise under her eye had nearly disappeared.

Nanny grabbed her purse and began digging around inside, finally
pulling out a tube of lipstick. She dabbed it on her lips and then handed
it to Mama.

Mama slowly dabbed the lipstick on her lips and handed it back to
Nanny.

"Here, sweet girl, we can't forget about you.", Nanny smiled and
bent down towards me. She gently dabbed the lipstick on my lips,
"Now, remember to smack.", she said as I nodded and then smacked my
lips together just as I had seen her and Mama do.

"There you go.", she said in approval, "I think we're ready girls.", she
said to us. With that, we walked out of the house to get in the car.

As we drove into town, we were all silent. I sat in Mama's lap as
she gazed out the window. I wasn't sure where we were going and as we
drove on I became nervous for Nanny and Mama. I knew we were in
the middle of a war like Nanny had said so, I envisioned us driving out
into the middle of nowhere and joining soldiers taking aim. I imagined
a lady being our leader yelling out orders to Nanny and Mama. I hoped
they'd make it out alive and started to wonder what would happen to
me if they didn't.

Eventually, my mind was put to ease when we ended up in front of
a building downtown that looked different from the other buildings on
the street. It was red bricked with some of them starting to crumble.
There were two picture windows in the front with one that had been
boarded up from what looked to be broken with a rock. A small hole
with cracks in the window covered the outside of the board that had
been placed on the other side. There was a faded white sign on the front
of the building with black letters that were becoming hard to see. As we
walked up, something told me by the looks on Mama and Nanny's faces
that there was not much hope behind the big wooden door that waited
for us to open. I was just relieved to see that there were no soldiers
around and no sounds of gunshots being fired.

Mama looked over at Nanny, "Are you sure this is the right place?", she asked.

Nanny took a few steps back and looked up at the address above the door. She pulled out a piece of paper from her purse and looked at it, then back again at the door.

She shrugged her shoulders, "Four, zero, nine, yep, that's what I have. Let's go on in and see.", she answered as she put her arm behind Mama, nudging her to the door. Mama grabbed my hand and pulled the door handle to open the door. Nanny followed behind us as the door pushed itself closed behind us with a loud creak.

Just inside was a woman sitting at a desk with piles of papers surrounding her. Some of the papers were shoved into folders while others were in messy stacks. The woman behind the desk looked up at us as we walked in, "Well, hello there.", she said with a smile. Her dark brown hair with strands of gray was pulled back out of her round face. She wore red lipstick and gold rimmed cat eye glasses. There was a mole above her top lip that I couldn't take my eyes off of as she spoke, "What can I do for you ladies?".

I waited for Nanny to tell the woman we were here to report for battle.

Instead, Nanny answered, "We're here to see Ms. Welch. We have an appointment.".

"Oh, ok.", the woman said as she opened a notebook, ran her finger down the page and the next page where she stopped, tapping the page and looking closer to read, "Mabel? Mabel Mair, is that right?".

"Yes, ma'am. ", Mama answered while Nanny nodded.

The woman stood up from behind her desk, "Alright, if you'll have a seat over there I'll let her know you're here.", the woman pointed to three mismatched chairs that sat beside a water fountain. Two chairs were metal with black covered cushions that had tears in them. I chose the big burgundy sofa chair to climb into. I traced my finger over the gold paisley design on the arm of the chair while we waited for the woman to return.

Mama looked around at the old paintings on the walls around us that had pictures of farms and pastures, "How did you find this lady?", Mama whispered to Nanny.

"I called around. It'll be fine.", Nanny answered and then patted Mama on the leg, "A woman might understand what we're dealing with better than a man.", she added.

Just then the woman from the desk returned with another woman following behind her. This woman was tall and thin, wearing a light blue dress with a collar that reminded me of a nurse's dress. She had long blonde hair that laid on her shoulders in big curls, pinned back out of her face.

"Mrs. Mair?", she asked as she stood in front of Mama with her hand out. Mama and Nanny stood up as Mama reached out to shake the woman's hand.

"Yes, ma'am, Mabel. Mabel Mair.", Mama answered.

"Wanda Welch, nice to meet you.", the woman said with a smile as they shook hands.

She turned to look at Nanny, "And you must be Peggy.", reaching out to shake Nanny's hand as well.

Nanny shook her hand confidently answering, "Yes, ma'am.".

"Come this way.", the woman pointed.

Mama picked me up out of the chair I was sitting in and followed the woman down a hall into an office with Nanny right behind us.

The office was a big room with two big bookshelves filled with books behind a desk where the woman sat. There was nothing but a folder on her desk, an empty ashtray and an antique lamp that had a colorful glass shade.

"Please, sit down.", the woman pointed at two brown leather chairs that faced the front of her desk. As Mama and Nanny sat down the leather chairs made a squeaky sound. Mama sat me in her lap and wrapped her arms around me.

"Tell me what's going on.", the woman started as she opened the folder on her desk and took out a pen from the drawer.

"I see you're trying to get your sons back? Is that right?", she said looking up from the open folder.

Mama nodded slowly as she spoke a whispered, "Yes, that's right.".

The woman smiled and opened the desk drawer, "Would you like some gum?", she asked Mama.

Mama shook her head, "No, thank you.", she responded.

The woman took out a package of gum and held it up to offer it to Nanny who reached over the desk and grabbed a piece.

"What about you?", the woman looked at me and then Mama, "Can she have some?", she asked.

I looked up at Mama hoping she'd say yes. She looked down at my eyes that were begging her to let me have a piece, "Sure, she can have a piece.", Mama nodded at me.

I jumped out of Mama's lap and excitedly grabbed a piece of gum from the woman. Maybe Nanny and Mama wouldn't be fighting in a battle today after all, I thought as I crawled back into Mama's lap. Feeling more comfortable now, I took the silver wrapper off of the piece of gum and pushed it into my mouth quickly as Mama held out her hand for me to deposit the wrapper.

The woman sat back in her chair, "Mabel, you can trust me, I'm here for you and it seems like your mother is too.", she glanced over at Nanny who nodded.

"So, tell me what you need from me.", the woman said as she sat back up, folding her hands on her desk with the pen between her fingers, "I understand your husband has some of your children?", she asked.

Mama nodded as she began to speak quietly, "Yes, he has our three sons and now he wants a divorce.".

The woman started writing in the folder as Mama spoke.

"Do you know his lawyer?", she asked Mama.

"Yes, Mr. Thompson. Dwayne Thompson.", Mama answered.

"He's quite the fellow.", Nanny commented as she rolled her eyes and shook her head.

The woman looked over at Nanny and nodded as if to agree with her.

"So, I'm guessing you've had experience with him?", she asked Nanny.

Nanny chewed her gum as she spoke with dissatisfaction about him, "Let's just say he's let me down a time or two and at this point he's no one to be trusted.".

The woman listened to Nanny and then drew her attention back to Mama.

"Ok, so, Mabel, I know this might be difficult, but I need to know as many details as possible. How did your husband end up with your sons?", she held her pen to the paper in the folder ready to write as soon as Mama started talking.

"Well, we got into an argument over a piece of paper he found with a number on it.", I felt Mama's fingers begin to run through the hair on the back of my head as she spoke softly.

"I tried to tell him it was the plumber's number but he didn't believe me.", Mama stopped her fingers and then paused looking at her other hand, spinning the wedding ring on her finger with her thumb.

"It got a little hard to talk to him...he was yelling.", Mama quieted her voice.

"Did he hurt you?", the woman asked, "I mean, did he ever hit you or anything like that?".

Mama looked over at Nanny looking for an answer other than the one she had to tell.

Mama loved Daddy and never told anyone but Nanny when he would hit her. She protected him with excuses while we watched her ice bruises or dab ointment on cuts. She would tell us kids it was an accident or that he didn't mean to, that she had just made Daddy really mad.

Telling someone she'd just met was like torture for her.

"Oh, come on, Mabel, spit it out.", Nanny spoke sternly, " It's not about Mike anymore, it's about your boys.".

Mama looked down and stared at the back of my head.

Slowly, Mama began to speak again, " Yes, I made him mad...so he slapped me.", Mama wrapped her arms around me, "I was upset so I left. Daisy was up so I took her with me...but the boys were asleep.".

Her arms gently squeezed around me as she retold what had happened, "We tried to go get them the next morning and he wouldn't let us.".

The woman stopped writing to look up at Mama, "Ok, so, what we have is a battered wife which means you have every right to move forward with this divorce and get custody of your sons. I can draw up some papers and we will ask for the boys to be handed back to you.".

Mama quickly sat up to argue, "Oh, no ma'am, I'm not a battered wife.".

Nanny stood up, "Mabel Ann!," she scolded, "There's no reason to protect him anymore.".

Walking over to a little black waste basket in the corner of the room, Nanny threw the gum she had been chewing into it and then pulled out a cigarette from her purse. Sticking it between her lips, ready to light, "May I?", she asked the woman who pushed the ashtray on her desk towards Nanny.

Mama rested her forehead in her hand and sighed.

"Mabel, it's important for me to know if Mr. Mair has a history of abuse with you.", the woman said, laying the pen down on the desk.

Mama looked over at Nanny and then at me still chewing the gum in my mouth. I looked up at Mama and smiled. Reaching up with my hand I stroked her cheek, "It ok Mama.", I tried to console her.

Mama gave me a little hug as a tear rolled down her cheek.

Mama wiped the tear with her hand and looked up at the woman, confident this time, "I am not a battered wife. I am a loving wife who respects her husband and right now I just want to have my boys with me."

Nanny threw her arms up in the air, "Battered wives go to their mother's house with bruises on their eyes!".

Nanny sat back down in the chair, flicked the ashes of her cigarette into the ashtray and looked over at Mama, "Mabel, please don't let that son of a...", she paused as her eyes locked with mine, "Don't let that man win.", she finished.

"Ok, let's all calm down.", the woman interrupted, "So, Mabel, if Mr. Mair wasn't abusive then we can simply go forward with the divorce as it is in his papers.", she flipped through some papers that were inside the folder on her desk.

"Alright then.", Mama agreed.

Nanny let out a huff and slumped back in her chair, crossing her arms.

"So what he's saying is that you abandoned your sons and for that he wants custody, giving you weekend visits.", the woman read the paper in the folder as she spoke.

"I did not abandon them. They were sleeping when I left and I went back for them the next morning. I would like to turn that around where I have custody.", Mama sat up straight, adjusting me in her lap.

The woman looked at Mama, " Well, we can try but I'm not sure if a judge will agree.", she answered back.

"Also, what about this little one?", the woman pointed to me, "Is she his child?", she asked.

"Yes, she's his child.", Mama said with a snap in her tone, "Mike just doesn't take too well to little girls.".

"Ok, well then I'll get the paperwork started and call you when I'm finished.", the woman said as she stood from her chair. Mama and Nanny both stood up as Mama picked me up into her arms. They shook hands with the woman and as we began to leave, the woman said behind us, "And, Mabel...", Mama turned back to look at her, "If you change your mind after you've had some time to think, all you have to do is call.", she finished.

Without an answer, Mama nodded and we walked out of the office to the car with Nanny marching out, clenching her purse, way ahead of us.

As Nanny started the car and began down the street she started in on Mama.

"Mabel, I don't understand why you protected him in there after all he's done to you.", she said, "These are your children we're talking about.".

"Yes, Mother, and one day those children will read those papers.", Mama raised her voice, "I want them to see that I didn't fight dirty.".

Nanny shook her head in disagreement,"But sometimes you have to get dirty to win the battle.", she raised her voice over Mama's.

Mama quit talking and stared out of the window, twirling her hair with her finger.

Nanny glanced over at Mama as she reached up to adjust the rearview mirror.

She rubbed her forehead and said, "Mabel, I love you more than life itself and I'll always support you even if I don't agree.", she reached over to grab Mama's hand, "We can't fight right now. Us girls have to stick together so we don't fall apart.".

Nanny glanced over at me, "Isn't that right, Daisy?", she asked.

I nodded and then rested my head on Mama's chest as we continued back to Nanny's.

Mama meandered through the next few days which turned into weeks with me following right along. Most days she began going out into Nanny's old shed in the backyard. There, she would sit at an easel and paint. The shed became her space. She kept the big barn-like door open and painted pictures of the sky or the wildflowers that dotted the yard. I'd stay busy playing nearby but would quickly get bored. It wasn't the same without my brothers. The best thing I knew to do by myself was to play in the big tractor tire filled with sand. I spent most of my time there attempting to make sandcastles with a bucket or sandcakes in an old tin pan Nanny let me have.

Nanny would take her creations she'd been working on to the town market to sell. Her newest items were birdcages she had made out of old wires and springs. She'd paint them and then hang them around to dry in the big foresty trees that surrounded the shed.

"You should take some of your paintings down there, Mabel.", she suggested to Mama, "You could make good money off of those beautiful masterpieces of yours.".

"Oh, I don't know, Mom, I just paint to keep my mind busy.", Mama told her.

"Well, think about it. People love one of a kind things.", Nanny went on, "It would give you something else to do and you could get to know some of the people down there."

Mama shrugged the idea off and promised Nanny she'd think about it.

It had been some time since we saw the woman in the office. Mama and Nanny would stay up talking in the kitchen after I went to bed. Mama and I slept together in the guest room. I loved sharing the bed with her, tucked up next to her each night. I was never able to sleep in Mama and Daddy's bed even when I woke up scared from a bad dream. She'd always get up and carry me back to bed where she would lay with me until I fell back to sleep.

Here, at Nanny's, I felt safe sleeping next to Mama.

One night, while lying in bed, I overheard Nanny and Mama talking.

"Bertie is going to come with us Monday so she can sit with Daisy.", Nanny said.

Bertie was Mama's older sister. We didn't see her much and Daddy always rolled his eyes when her name came up in conversations with Mama.

She was different from Mama, short and pudgy with wavy brown hair that she kept tucked behind her ears. Bertie didn't seem to mind how she looked, always wearing long plain colored dresses with a light yellow sweater she knitted herself. Bertie never wore makeup like Mama.

Her and Mama never seemed to agree on things, but always ended their discussions with a hug and an, "I'll see you again.", before leaving.

"Ok, that'll be good.", Mama responded to Nanny.

"We're going to be fine and when it's all said and done you'll have your boys back where they belong.", Nanny added.

"I hope so. Everyone in town knows Mr. Thompson though.", Mama said with a sigh.

"Well that's true, but Ms. Welch is young and new. Men like shiny, new things. Especially when it's a woman.", Nanny chuckled.

"Oh, I just can't wait to see their little faces again and hold them. This time I'm never letting them go.", Mama said.

"You will, honey, just you wait and see.", Nanny told her.

As I laid there that night after listening in on Mama and Nanny's conversation, I thought about my brothers. I missed playing with Marc and Mitch and I missed following Matt around, trying to do everything he did. I wondered if they were missing me too.

Then, I thought about Daddy. Did he miss me? Did he miss Mama?

As much as I wanted to be with my brothers again, I had really enjoyed the time away from Daddy.

It was nice not to hear him grumbling and besides, I didn't think he liked me anyway. He barely ever spoke to me unless he was telling me to do something or to be quiet. I couldn't remember the last time he held me in his arms or stopped to notice anything I was doing.

Maybe Mama and Nanny were talking about us going home. I wasn't sure why Bertie would need to sit with me though, except maybe for Mama and Daddy to talk. The word divorce had been coming up a lot in their conversations but I wasn't sure what it meant. Since Dad wanted it, I decided maybe a divorce was a kind of dessert. I imagined him eating a big chocolate cake with lots of chocolate syrup on top, especially after I'd heard Nanny one time say he wanted his cake and eat it too.

Maybe this time when Daddy says he's sorry he'll mean it since it had been longer than usual for us to be gone. I imagined him hugging Mama, telling her he wouldn't get mad like that again. Then I imagined him picking me up, telling me he loved me and, for the first time, calling me by my name. Maybe this time would be different.

After he tells Mama he's sorry and eats his cake I could run outside and finally play with my brothers again.

Chapter Ten- (Matt)

It had felt so long since I'd seen Mama. The more time went by, the angrier I became while Dad seemed to be getting happier.

He had started going out more nights than he was home, with Aunt Becky still coming to sit with us. Some nights he even stayed out until the next morning. Everytime, going dressed in his best clothes with his hair neatly combed down to the side.

We didn't talk about Mama or Daisy much anymore as life went on without them.

When either of them came to my mind I tried my best to push the thoughts of them out.

The next time Aunt Becky had come over after I hit her, I knew I needed to apologize in some way but I wasn't sure how. I stood in the hallway as she walked in the front door that night feeling shameful because I knew I had hurt her. As she closed the door behind her, Marc and Mitch went running down the hall, pushing past me.

"Aunt Becky!", they squealed as they ran up to hug her.

She laughed as they swaddled her with their arms in excitement.

"Okay, okay.", she giggled as she hugged them back, "What are you all doing up so late?", she smiled as they both followed her to the couch where she sat.

"We wanted to see you.", Marc answered, climbing into her lap.

"Yeah, we want to see you.", Mitch repeated, climbing to join Marc in her lap.

They snuggled up close to her as she wrapped her arms around them.

I continued watching from the hallway unsure if she would even want me around after what I'd done to her.

She kissed the top of Mitch's head as he stuck his thumb in his mouth, her eyes drifted over to where I was still standing.

"Hey, Matt, you ok?", she spoke softly over the tops of my brothers' heads.

Did she forget how I treated her last time?, I thought.

"Do you want a hug?", she asked.

In disbelief that she would even want to talk to me again, I slowly walked closer to where she was sitting. As I got closer to her, she stuck out her hand from around Marc, waving me over. I scooted in next to Marc and squeezed in close, becoming a part of the human sandwich they had created. I felt her hand rub the top of my head and then move down to squeeze my shoulder. Without having to say anything at all, she let me know she had already forgiven me.

"You guys want me to make some popcorn?", she asked.

The three of us looked up at her excitedly and nodded our heads.

Aunt Becky was old enough to drive but still in high school. She looked a lot like Dad with her deep set, dark brown eyes and "Mair point" in her nose. Her dark hair was always pulled back into a ponytail and she had a small dimple in the side of her chin.

As much as I was trying to forget about Mama, Aunt Becky made it feel as though she was there.

She giggled as we played, colored in coloring books with us and always took care of some of the chores around the house. Although the way she washed the dishes and put away our clothes was different from the way Mama had done it, it was nice to know somebody wanted to take care of us.

Aunt Becky loved Elvis Presley. In fact, she loved him so much she had all of his records and brought them over sometimes to play them on our record player. She had even been to one of his concerts when he came to Detroit. When she would play her favorite song, Blue Suede Shoes, we would twist our hips to dance along and I would practice shuffling my knees like I had seen him do on t.v. We had our own dance party all together right there in the living area. Aunt Becky made things feel easy, so the more she came to sit with us the more I tried replacing Mama with her. Everytime I hugged her, I closed my eyes and imagined Mama. It was the only time I let myself not be angry with her.

I wasn't sure where Dad was spending all of his time in the evenings, but wherever it was seemed to be helping him. Not only was he drinking less, he had started waking us up in the mornings for school with less of a holler and a few times when he came home from work he had started bringing us each a piece of a candy.

He still wasn't much of a talker, so most evenings we all sat quietly at the table to eat supper.

"How was school?", he'd ask as we ate whatever he had scrounged up for us, which usually ended up as some kind of sandwich.

"Good.", I'd answer. He never asked anymore than that so I knew that's all he really wanted to hear.

One night, I overheard him talking on the phone as I was laying in bed.

"This will all be over soon, honey, and then we'll be together.", he said.

Is he talking to Mama?, I wondered.

I've never heard him call her honey before., I thought to myself.

I laid there trying as hard as I could to breathe as slowly and quietly as possible so I could hear what he was saying.

"I can't wait either.", he continued, "After Monday this will be past us and you can finally be here with us.".

It has to be Mama., I thought, Who else could it be?.

At that moment, I wasn't sure how to feel about Mama coming back. I was so angry with her for leaving us behind and for so long, but I also missed her so much. I closed my eyes and dreamed of her.

When Monday came, Dad was already dressed when he woke us up for school. He was wearing a black suit jacket and tie with a white button up shirt. I'd only ever seen him wear this suit when he went to my grandfather's funeral.

I rubbed my eyes and asked, "Dad, are you going to a funeral?".

He chuckled and answered, "Well, I guess you could say that.".

As he walked out of our bedroom he whistled a tune. I'd never heard him whistle like that, in fact, I didn't even know he could whistle.

I stumbled out of bed to begin getting ready for school.

It's Monday. I thought as I remembered Dad's conversation on the phone. I quickly got dressed and nudged Marc and Mitch to get out of bed, "Come on you guys.", I hurried them out of bed to get dressed. I dug through Mitch's clothes that Aunt Becky had placed in the drawer. Grabbing the first pants and shirt I saw, I tossed them to Mitch.

My heart was pounding and my body was moving quicker than I could think as I thought about Mama coming back.

I couldn't wait to get to school and get back home to her. I imagined her standing at the door with Daisy, waiting for us to get home, smiling and then running to hold us in her arms. She would smother us with kisses and tell us she's sorry for leaving us behind. Everything would finally be back to normal once I got home from school.

When I walked into the kitchen, Dad was still whistling as he poured milk into three bowls of cereal.

I sat down at the table, watching him, I'd never seen him act like this.

He placed one of the bowls of cereal in front of me on the table and happily patted my head.

"Marcus! Mitchell!", he hollered out and set the other two bowls on the table across from me. He walked away down the hallway to hurry them.

I began shoveling cereal into my mouth as if I only had a few seconds to eat.

Marc and Mitch came bouncing down the hall and into the kitchen while Dad chased behind them trying to tickle them. They giggled all the way to the table quickly sitting down in front of the bowls of cereal.

I didn't understand Dad's unusual behavior, but decided he must be as excited as I was to have Mama back.

Maybe this time he'll quit hitting her like he always promises her., I thought as I slurped up the milk in my bowl.

When we eventually left the house for school, Dad handed us each a nickel for milk and patted us on the heads, "Alright, you guys, have a good day.", he said to us as we started down the sidewalk.

It has to be Mama., I thought as I began skipping down the street excited to get the school day over with so I could get back home to her.

"Matt! Wait up!", I heard Marc call from behind me.

I stopped to look back, "Come on, you guys!", I hollered back to him and Mitch as they were running to catch up to me.

We stopped in front of Jake's house to wait for him to come out and walk with us.

When he came out of his front door he ran to meet up with us.

We gave each other a slap handshake like always as we began our walk to school.

"Guess what?", I asked Jake excitedly.

"You're really a girl?", he laughed as he answered.

I reached over and softly slugged him in the shoulder, "No, numb nuts.", I replied.

Jake rubbed his shoulder, "Well then, what?", he giggled.

"My mom's coming home!", I said almost in a shout.

"See, I told you she'd be back.", he said.

Marc and Mitch who were trailing behind us came running to catch up.

"Did you say Mama's coming home?", Marc asked me as he tugged on my shirt.

I nodded my head at him and smiled, "Yes! She'll be waiting for us after school today.", I answered.

"Mama!", Mitch hollered.

"Oh, boy! I can't wait!", Marc said, "Come on. Mitchie, let's hurry!".

They grabbed hands and began running in front of Jake and I.

As I watched them run ahead, for the first time since Mama had left, it felt like today was going to be a good day.

I patted Jake on the back, "Come on, slow poke, let's catch up.", I said with a smile as we ran to catch up to my brothers.

Chapter Eleven- (Daisy)

When Monday came, Mama and Nanny were up earlier than usual.

As I opened my eyes and rolled over to feel the empty space in the bed where Mama had been laying, I could hear the two of them bustling around.

"I can't find it anywhere.", I heard Mama say.

"Oh, calm down, Mabel, it's here somewhere.", Nanny assured her.

I could hear Mama shuffling through things in the hall closet.

I decided to get out of bed and help Mama.

"What you looking for, Mama?", I asked.

"Oh, just something for your brothers.", she answered without looking up. She continued pulling out boxes and bags filled with different things like scraps of ribbon and cloth, old newspapers and shiny wrapping paper. Then she shoved it all back into the closet and closed the door.

Looking over at me she said, "Good mornin', you're up early.".

She walked over to me and picked me up, giving me a hug. As she carried me into the kitchen, she kissed me on the cheek and gently pushed a strand of hair out of my face.

"Sorry, baby, we don't have time to make breakfast this morning, so cereal will have to do.", she sat me down in a chair at the kitchen table and went to the cabinet to grab a box of Wheaties.

Just then, Nanny came down the hall dressed in a black dress with thin white stripes that fit tight to her thin body. With it she wore black heels and a pearl necklace. Her hair in curls around her face, she was carrying a brown paper sack in her hand, "Found it!", she exclaimed as she walked into the kitchen.

"Oh, well good mornin', baby girl.", she said to me and then patted me on the head. She sat the sack on the table, "Didn't I tell you it would turn up?", she patted Mama on the back as Mama rushed over to the table.

"Look, Daisy.", she pulled out three small, light brown teddy bears each with a different colored bow around its neck, one blue, one red and one green.

"I got these for your bubbas when we get to see them today.", she told me as she sat each one on the table and smoothed out each of their bows.

She rubbed each bears' face and looked at them longingly.

With a mouthful of cereal I said, "Oh, pretty, Mama, I like them.".

"And of course, I didn't forget about you.", she smiled as she pulled one more teddy bear out of the sack. This one had a pink bow around its neck.

"For me, Mama?", I asked excitedly.

She nodded her head and handed me the bear. I took it in my arms and gave it a hug, "Thank you, Mama.".

"Oh, you're welcome, baby. I love you so, so much.", she kissed the top of my head.

"Okay, now, I need to finish getting ready.", she said as she put the bears back into the sack and walked away.

Mama eventually came back out wearing a light blue maxi dress and her hair pinned back in curls. Nanny had dressed me in a pink frilly dress with pink bows on the shoulders. I wasn't sure why we all needed to get so dressed up to go back home.

As we walked to the door, Nanny pulled her lipstick out of her purse, dabbed it on her lips and handed it to Mama. They both looked in the mirror beside the door and smacked their lips.

Nanny bent down to dab some lipstick on my lips, "Remember what to do?", she asked.

I smacked my lips, "Good girl.", she smiled.

When we were finally in the car and headed down the street, I could feel the nervousness rise. Mama was shaking her foot and twirling her hair around her finger while she gazed out the window. Nanny sat straight up in her seat as she drove and I sat in between them, eager to see my brothers. The brown paper sack with the bears was in the backseat.

"Alright, Daisy, now you are going to sit with Bertie and be a good girl while Mama and I handle some business.", Nanny told me.

I nodded my head still wondering why Bertie needed to sit with me.

We pulled up in front of a big white brick building with lots of stories and windows.

Mama took a big breath and let it out, "I sure hope Ms. Welch knows what she's doing.", Mama whispered.

"Me too, honey, me too.", said Nanny.

For the first time the most confident woman in the world seemed a little fragile.

Nanny patted Mama on the leg, "Let's go on in.", she told her. Mama reached down and squeezed Nanny's hand.

The three of us got out of the car and began walking along the sidewalk up to the building.

Waiting at the front door was Bertie in a plain mint green dress and her yellow knitted sweater, carrying a black purse.

She smiled as we walked up to meet her. No one spoke, they only nodded at each other and patted each other's backs. "Hi, Daisy.", Bertie said to me as she reached for my hand.

I grabbed her hand and we walked into the building behind Mama and Nanny.

There was a policeman standing at the door to greet us, "Morning ladies.", he said to us, tipping his hat. Nanny and Mama nodded at him.

Inside, was a big, wide hallway with lots of doors on one side and a long counter on the opposite side. There were benches sitting on the outside of each door. Big painted pictures of gray and white haired men wearing black robes hung in rows on each side of the hallway walls. Bertie and I sat down on a bench while Mama and Nanny went up to the counter where a red headed woman sat. They spoke quietly to each other and the woman pointed towards one of the doors.

As Mama and Nanny turned to come back to where Bertie and I sat we heard a voice coming from down the hall, "Mrs. Mair, Ms. Culhane.". It was the woman from the office, Ms. Welch. She walked quickly to where we were with a folder full of papers in her hand and a black satchel hanging from her shoulder. Her blonde hair was pulled back into a bun and she was wearing a very important looking black dress. The kind I'd seen the president's wife wear on t.v.

"Good morning.", she said as she shook both Mama and Nanny's hands, "The judge should be ready for us soon.".

As the women began talking, I looked over at the front door and saw the big round man, Mr. Thompson, walking inside. Behind him was Daddy in a suit and tie.

"Daddy.", I whispered.

Bertie, who was still sitting next to me on the bench, turned to look towards the front door. She stood up quickly when she spotted him and stood in front of me as if she were a guard.

Once they passed the policeman at the front door, Daddy glanced past me and towards Mama as he and Mr. Thompson stopped by the wall and stood there to talk.

The door beside the bench I was sitting on swung open and a sheriff walked out. He propped the door open, "Parties for the matter of Mrs. Mabel Mair and Mr. Michael Mair.", he said as he pointed inside the door.

Mama looked down as she walked inside the doorway with Daddy behind her along with Mr. Thompson and Ms. Welch. Nanny blew me a kiss as she followed behind them inside the room.

Maybe Daddy will get his cake in there. Maybe that's why we're all dressed up, because it's a party.

When the door closed behind them all, Bertie sat back down on the bench beside me. She put her arm around me and I leaned into her side.

"Where are my bubbas?", I asked.

"Oh, you know, they're at school.", Bertie answered.

"Is Daddy having chocolate cake?", I asked.

Bertie looked down at me, "Cake?", she sounded confused.

"You know, Daddy's eating cake in the party.", I pointed to the closed door that Mama and Daddy had entered.

Bertie let out a quiet chuckle, "Oh girl, you've got quite the imagination now, don't you?".

I wasn't sure what she meant by that so it made me wonder if Bertie even knew about the party.

"Is Daddy taking me and Mama home today?", I asked.

Bertie patted my knee, "You sure ask a lot of questions.".

I leaned my head back into her side, deciding that Bertie must not know much of anything.

As the two of us waited, there on the bench, I watched as people walked by. Most of them were men, all dressed up in suits, carrying papers or satchels. All of them looked angry with frowns on their faces and lines in their foreheads. One woman in a pink dress walked by and smiled at me as she passed.

As I watched people coming and going down the big hall in front of us, I thought about my brothers.

I couldn't wait to see them. Maybe me and Mama are going to surprise them., I thought. She'll give them each the teddy bears she brought for them and we'll all go inside the house to get ready for supper.

As I sat there with Bertie thinking about it all, I began to doze off.

I wasn't sure how long I had been sleeping when I heard the door open. Daddy came out first with Mr. Thompson behind him, patting him on the back. They were both smiling as they walked right past me.

"Daddy!", I called to him as they began walking down the hall.

Maybe he didn't see me., I thought as I called a little louder, "Daddy!", quickly standing up thinking that would help him see me.

As he continued walking away I shouted this time, "Daddy!", with all my might so he could hear me.

For a moment, he turned back to look at me as he kept walking and we locked eyes.

He saw me!, I thought and waited for him to turn around and come back to me.

Instead, he turned his head as if he didn't know me and kept walking until he was out of sight.

My heart sank at the realization that Daddy didn't recognize me.

I decided he must have forgotten what I looked like since he hadn't seen me in so long.

What if my bubbas forgot what I look like too?, I worried as I slumped back down beside Bertie.

Next, out of the door came Mama who was practically being carried by Nanny with her arms wrapped around Mama. Ms. Welch followed behind them with her hand on Mama's back.

Mama stumbled as she walked, "Sit here for a minute.", Nanny told Mama as she helped her sit down beside me on the bench.

Mama slouched over with her head in her hands and cried loudly, echoing down the big hallway.

I couldn't imagine why she was so upset as I sat wide eyed watching her.

Nanny and Ms. Welch whispered some words to each other and then said goodbye. Ms. Welch looked sadly at me and walked away still carrying her satchel.

"What in the world happened in there?", Bertie asked.

Nanny leaned down to rub Mama's back and shook her head to respond with a no to Bertie.

I put my whole body over the back of Mama trying to help Nanny console her.

Hugging her with my arms around her back, she reached around and pulled me to the front of her and held me in her lap, holding me tight.

Her cries began to slow and soften as she caught her breath.

"Come on, honey, let's get out of here.", Nanny said as she helped Mama stand up.

She walked alongside Mama all the way to the car while Bertie held my hand following them.

"I just can't believe it.", Bertie said as Mama slid into the car.

"It's an utter disgrace.", Nanny replied as she helped me into the car.

Nanny talked to Bertie outside of the car while I crawled up next to Mama's side.

"Did Daddy not like his cake?", I asked Mama.

Mama looked over at me confused and pulled me into her lap without speaking, still sobbing.

When Nanny got in the car, we rode silently along with the teddy bears still in the brown paper sack setting in the backseat, all the way back to Nanny's, not home to Daddy and without my brothers.

Chapter Twelve- (Matt)

The school bell rang as I ran outside to find Marc and Mitch in front of the school. As soon as I saw them I hollered, "Come on!", and began running towards home. They came running to catch up behind me shouting, "Matt, wait up!".

My legs couldn't run fast enough as I couldn't wait any longer to get home.

"Let's go you two!", I hollered back at them. Running down the sidewalk, I started to lose my breath. It wasn't until I had finally reached our street when I slowed down to a walk. If I got home without my brothers I'd be in trouble so I looked back and impatiently shouted for them to hurry.

When they caught up to me Mitch asked, "Is Mama home?".

"She's supposed to be.", I answered as we continued walking quickly.

As we approached our house I noticed that Mama's car wasn't in the driveway next to Dad's.

Maybe Dad picked her up., I thought, I bet her car is still at Nanny's.

We got to the front door of our house and I nearly burst into tears with excitement to see Mama. I imagined opening the door and seeing her standing inside waiting for us.

I pushed the door open and walked inside with Marc and Mitch behind me. The house was silent and empty.

"Mama? Daisy?", I called out and began walking from room to room looking for them. Marc and Mitch, still behind me, echoed their names after me.

Quickly, I realized they were nowhere to be found inside the house. I turned to walk back to the living area as I could feel heat rising from my stomach to my chest. Holding in tears, I pushed Marc as I walked past him, "Get out of my way.", I grumbled.

I plopped down on the couch and crossed my arms as anger began to rise, fueled from disappointment.

Marc and Mitch sat down next to me on the couch, "Where are they? Where's Mama?", Marc asked.

"How should I know, nimwit?", I snapped.

Marc didn't say another word and Mitch began quietly sobbing, sticking his thumb in his mouth.

Just then, Dad came inside from the backdoor. Alone, with a white t-shirt and jeans that had replaced his suit and tie from the morning, he walked into the living room to see the three of us sitting on the couch. None of us moved as we saw that neither Mama or Daisy were with him. Instead, we sat there frozen in confusion of what we were feeling, not understanding where Mama was.

"What's the matter with you guys?", he asked.

"Nothing.", I whispered and slowly got up to go to my room. Behind me I heard Dad tell Mitch, "Get that out of your mouth, boy, and what are you crying about?".

I climbed onto my bed and angrily punched my pillow. I had never felt so mad, so disappointed.

As I used my pillow to take out my frustration, I decided right then and there that I would not be disappointed again. I would decide soon which of the two not to trust anymore, Mama or Dad.

Dad didn't say much of anything the rest of the evening until Aunt Becky showed up as he was about to leave.

"How'd it go?", she asked Dad as she came in and set down her purse.

"Oh, you know, exactly how I expected it to go.", he answered, "She had nothing to prove and I had everything.", he smiled in accomplishment.

She dropped her shoulders, looking over at the three of us boys who were now sitting at the table eating peanut butter and jelly sandwiches.

"So, what about Daisy?", she asked.

Interested to hear more about what they were talking about, I focused intently on my sandwich so as not to look like I was listening. I began chewing slowly in order to make sure I heard them clearly.

Dad looked over at us and then at Aunt Becky, "Oh, I won that too. Her little lady of a lawyer was no match for Mr. Thompson."

He grabbed his keys off of the hook by the front door and waved, "I'll be back later on.", he said as he left.

Aunt Becky came into the kitchen where we were sitting and began making herself a sandwich.

"Well, I guess that's that.", she said as she smoothed peanut butter onto two pieces of bread and then slapped them together.

"How was school today?", she asked us as she carried her sandwich over to join us at the table.

None of us answered.

"Why the glum faces?", she asked as she took a bite of her sandwich.

"Mama was supposed to come back.", Mitch said as he put his thumb in his mouth.

"Aunt Becky, do you know why Mama didn't come back today?", Marc asked as he sat back in his chair and pulled his knees up to his chest with his arms around them.

I stayed silent and as much as I wanted to know the answer too, I also didn't want to talk about it.

"Oh, she's with Daisy at your Nanny's.", she answered.

"Is she coming back?", Marc asked.

Aunt Becky began scooting in her chair and picked a piece of crust off of her bread.

"Umm, well, I don't...um.", she nervously began to answer as Marc and Mitch sat waiting for her response.

I didn't want to talk about this day anymore. With my hands, I used the table to shove my chair back, pushing the table which caused Mitch's glass of milk to knock over and spill onto the floor.

"Matthew!", shouted Aunt Becky while she got up from the table. After startling them all, I too got up from the table quickly and ran to my room as they watched.

I found a GI Joe that was laying on the bedroom floor and picked it up. I threw it across the room where it hit a lamp on the dresser as it flew, hitting the wall with a thud and falling to the ground. Clenching my fists, I looked around for something else to throw. The only thing around was a Batman comic book I had been reading, so I picked it up and threw it, but it didn't have the same effect as the GI Joe. Instead, it drifted slowly down to the floor landing open, facedown. I kicked it across the floor and sat on my bed. I wanted to be anywhere else but home right now.

I thought about what Dad had said, How did what go? What did he win? And what about the conversation I heard him having on the phone the other night? Wasn't he talking to Mama? Maybe it wasn't her after all.

I felt so confused as I thought, nothing seemed right and all I really wanted was Mama.

I laid down and curled into a ball, pulled the blanket over myself and cried myself to sleep.

Chapter Thirteen- (Daisy)

"Good mornin', baby girl.", Nanny said to me with a smile. I had just walked into the kitchen to find her.

"You want to help me make some biscuits?", she asked as she wiped her hands on her pink apron.

I nodded my head as she scooted a chair next to where she was working and lifted me into it. She rolled out a big ball of dough and then handed me a lid from a canning jar. I began pressing the lid into the dough creating perfectly shaped circles.

"That's right. Good girl.", Nanny said to me.

It had been a few days since the devastation of Monday had happened. Nanny and Mama hadn't spoken much about it around me, instead they wandered through the days with Mama seeming lost. She'd been back to sleeping most of the time and Nanny kept busy either with chores around the house or outside working on her creations.

"We've got to get your Mama to eat.", she said to me as I attempted to pull the dough away from around the circles. Reaching over to help, she added, "Sometimes, Daisy, this life sure hands out big surprises.".

"Are we having a 'prise today?", I asked.

"Well, let's just say we're working on having one soon.", she answered.

I couldn't imagine what the surprise we would be working on could be. Nanny took the tray of neatly cut dough circles and put them into the oven.

"Ok, we'll wait for those while I make us some eggs.", she said as she helped me out of the chair.

I went straight to my coloring book of farms while I waited.

Mama came down the hallway scratching her head and yawning.

"Good mornin', Mama.", I said to her.

In a slow, tired voice she responded, "Good mornin', sunshine.", as she walked into the kitchen and sat down at the table.

Nanny handed Mama a cup of coffee, "Okay, I been thinking. Maybe we should go together with all three of us.", she said as she went back to the eggs she was scrambling.

"I can sit in the car and wait.", she added.

Mama nodded her head as she sipped her coffee.

"Why won't he at least just see her?", Mama asked as she gazed at me over her coffee cup.

Nanny threw her hands in the air, waving the spatula, "Beats me. She's the most beautiful little girl, even with his eyes and nose. I can't for the life of me figure out how he could ever deny her.".

Mama let out a sigh, "I guess if he can say I abandoned my children and refused to come back for them, then he can say just about all he wants.".

"Well, that judge has a few screws loose, letting that man have custody of them after he blacked your eye.", Nanny added.

"I guess I should have fought dirty. I should have taken pictures like the judge asked about.", Mama said.

Nanny nodded as she turned off the stove and pulled the tray from the oven, "Well, honey, there's nothing we can do about all that now.", she said as she sat the tray of soft, golden biscuits on the counter. She pulled out three plates from the cabinet, scooped some eggs onto each one and then quickly tossed a hot biscuit onto the plates.

"First things first, we go over there and pick them up for your visitation.", she handed a fork to Mama, "Come on, Daisy, come eat these delicious looking biscuits you made.", she called to me.

"I'm sorry, Mom, I know you worked hard on all this. I'm just not hungry.", Mama said as I came to join them at the table. She poked her fork into the eggs and scooted them around on her plate with her head resting on her hand, like a child refusing to eat.

As Nanny smoothed butter onto a biscuit, "Well, okay, but you can't refuse these biscuits.", she smiled over at me and winked, "Baby girl made them herself.".

Mama put down her fork, "Oh, alright, I'll try one.", she picked the biscuit up off of her plate and took a bite.

"Is it good, Mama?", I asked as she chewed and then wiped her mouth with a napkin.

"Oh, it's not good...it's delicious!", Mama smiled at me.

Nanny looked over at me, "Well, Daisy, looks like we finally found the trick.", she took a bite of her biscuit and then with her mouth full she said, "I think we have a new cook for the kitchen.".

Later that day, we were headed for the front door when Mama came out carrying the brown paper sack that had the teddy bears in it, "Okay, Daisy, let's go see the boys.".

My heart started beating so fast I thought it might jump out of my chest, "Really, Mama?", I squealed and ran for the door, "Is that the 'prise, Nanny?", I asked eagerly as I followed the two of them out the door.

"Oh, hold on.", said Nanny as she dug through her purse to find her lipstick. We each quickly took turns rubbing it on our lips as we walked to the car.

As we drove, I excitedly sat in the front seat between them on my knees.

I couldn't wait to hug my brothers and tell them all about the town I'd created in the backyard sand. They would be so proud of me, especially Matt. Maybe we could even play together for a little bit.

When we got to the house, Daddy's car wasn't there. Nanny pulled into the driveway and parked, "Well, looks like he's not here.", she said to Mama, "Go on up and knock anyway. You never know.".

Mama pulled down the mirror on the visor and fluffed her curls, "Okay, here I go.", she said with a deep breath.

She carried the brown sack with her to the door and knocked. Nanny and I sat anxiously waiting and watching.

There was no answer and after a moment Mama knocked again. Standing there on the porch, she looked around, waiting. One more knock and then she stepped off of the porch and tried peeking in the front window. Nanny rolled down the window, "Well?", she asked, "Anything?".

Mama shook her head no and walked back to the car with her head down.

As she got back in, she slumped, defeated, in her seat.

"Well, we'll just have to come back later.", Nanny said, "He can't stay gone forever.".

My heart dropped as Nanny put the car in reverse and we drove away. I leaned over into Mama's side while she clutched the sack in her arms. She began crying as Nanny reached over and patted her leg.

Instead of going back to Nanny's we went downtown to an ice cream parlor.

"Maybe, this will help while we wait.", Nanny said to us.

Inside the ice cream parlor, Nanny and I stood at the counter in front of a large glass case with large tubs of different flavored ice cream in each.

"Hello ladies, what'll it be?", a very thin, red headed teenage boy wearing a white apron and paper hat asked.

"I don't think I'll have anything.", Mama said as she walked over to a booth to sit down.

Nanny lifted me up to see inside the case a little better, "What kind would you like, Daisy?", she asked me.

"I want chocut.", I answered and pointed.

"Alright, one scoop of chocolate and I'll have a scoop of vanilla, in cones please.", Nanny said to the boy as she put me back down.

Nanny and I carried our ice cream cones over to where Mama was sitting, leaned over, staring out the window beside her.

"He said I could get them at five o'clock.", Mama quietly said, still staring out the window.

"That's what he told the judge.", Nanny agreed as she licked her ice cream,

"Let's just try to enjoy our time here for now and then we'll go back.".

Nanny was right, the ice cream did help a little, at least for the moment.

Nanny finished her ice cream before me as chocolate began dripping down through my fingers. Trying to keep up with it, I licked the ice cream as fast as I could.

Nanny took her cigarettes out of her purse, offering one to Mama, she held the box out in front of her. Mama looked over at Nanny.

"It helps me.", Nanny said to her with a shrug.

Mama reached for a cigarette, Nanny lit the cigarette in her mouth and then held the lighter out for Mama to light the one she had grabbed.

I had never seen Mama smoke before, but if Nanny said it would help her, then it would.

They both sat there smoking and staring out the window while I finished my ice cream.

"You know, he had to have had some money stashed somewhere to afford Mr. Thompson.", Nanny pondered, "I knew Ms. Welch was cheap, but I hoped her being a woman would be in our favor.".

"I thought so too.", Mama said as she thumped ashes off of her cigarette into the ashtray on the table. A big puff of smoke blew into the air out of Mama's mouth as she added, "Instead, all those men in there saw her as a joke.".

Nanny began speaking in a deep voice, impersonating Mr. Thompson, "Well, I'm sorry, Ms. Welch, but why would she leave her boys with him if he was hitting on her? If she's got other men's phone numbers in her little black book, Mr. Mair has all the reason in the world to believe that little girl isn't his.", Nanny finished, letting out a frustrated chuckle.

Mama sat back and then put her cigarette out in the ashtray, "Men always win.".

Nanny took one last puff of her cigarette and put it out in the ashtray, "That's exactly why us girls have to stick together. Makes us stronger.", she added as she got up from the table and went to the lady's room. Chocolate was dripping from my fingers as I took the last bite of my cone. Nanny came back with wet paper napkins and began wiping me up, including my face.

"Alright, girls, let's go on back. It's been over an hour now.", she said as she helped me out of the booth and Mama scooted out of the side she had been sitting in.

When we got back to the house, there was a woman I had never seen before in the yard, watering the grass with the water hose. Nanny pulled up across the street from the house, "Who's that?", Nanny asked.

"I have no idea.", answered Mama.

The woman hadn't noticed us as we watched her spray the water onto the grass. She was tall and thin with long, dark hair, almost black. She was wearing a pink housecoat and no shoes. She had big, angry looking eyes and a long chin.

"Maybe she knows where they are.", Mama said as she got out of the car. She started to shut the door and then turned back, "I'm going to take Daisy. Maybe she'll help me when she sees a little one with me.". Nanny nodded as Mama reached in and swooped me up into her arms. She walked slowly across the street carrying me on her hip. When the woman noticed us she stopped spraying the water hose and walked towards the fence beside the sidewalk.

"Hello.", Mama said to her, waving her hand.

The woman stared at Mama as we got closer.

"What do you want?", the woman asked rudely with an accent I'd never heard before.

"Well, I'm here to see my sons and was wondering if they're home.", Mama answered.

"I know who you are. You're Mabel.", the woman sounded irritated, "You can go ahead and leave. Mike's not here and I'm not going to be responsible for giving the boys to you.", she said.

"Oh.", said Mama, surprised, "Well could I just see them real quick? I won't take them anywhere. Can they see their sister?", she asked as she put her hand on my chest.

"I'm not comfortable with that while he's not here, besides they're about to get ready for bed.", the woman replied in a quick, huffy tone.

As Mama and the woman talked, I saw the curtain move from inside the boys' bedroom window. There was a figure peeking out between the curtains.

It was Matt!

As our eyes locked I waved at him but he didn't respond.

"Okay, well, I'm supposed to have a visitation with them this weekend. Could you have Mike call me at my Mother's house when he gets home?", Mama asked.

"I'll tell him you came by.", the woman put her hand on her hip and turned to walk away.

"Thank you...", Mama paused, "What was your name?", she asked the woman who continued walking away, never answering as she went into the house.

Mama turned to go back to the car with me looking behind her over her shoulder. I kept my eyes on Matt, still in the window, I waved again, hoping he would wave back this time, but he didn't.

Chapter Fourteen- (Matt)

When we walked in from school on Wednesday, Dad was already home from work. He was sitting at the kitchen table holding hands with a woman I'd never seen before. She had long dark hair with a pointy nose and chin. Her eyes were big and round. There were deep dimples in her cheeks as she smiled when she saw us.

"Boys.", he let go of her hand and stood up from the table, "I'd like you to meet someone.", he pointed his hand in the woman's direction.

Marc and Mitch stood beside me as the woman stood up next to Dad. He put his arm around her and guided her closer to us, "This is Maria.", he said, beaming.

"Hi.", Mitch said shyly to her. Marc said nothing. I nodded hello and then plopped onto the couch.

"See there, it's all going to be fine.", Dad said to Maria as he kissed her forehead. He walked over to where I was sitting, patting Marc and Mitch on the head as he passed by them.

I was sitting with my arms crossed, trying to understand what was going on. Nothing made sense anymore.

"Can I go out and play?," I asked as Dad sat down next to me.

He nodded and said, "Be in when I call you.".

I quickly got up and ran outside. I ran as fast as I could, as if I were running from a burning building. Stopping at Jake's house, I leaned over to catch my breath before knocking on the door.

Jake came out carrying his baseball and two mitts.

"Come on, you're so slow.", I told him as he walked towards me.

"What's your problem?", he asked.

"Oh, come on, are we going or not?", I snapped.

"Alright, alright.", he said as he handed me a mitt.

We began walking to the baseball field as I searched my mind for something to talk about other than what was happening at home. I asked, "What did you get on that stupid book report?".

"Oh, I got an A. What about you?", he began skipping ahead of me.

"An A? I got a C.", I answered and began jogging behind him.

"Oh, is that your problem? A C?", he laughed, "Well, come on. We don't have long before supper.", he trotted onto the field.

There, on the field, all I had to focus on was catching the ball and throwing it back.

As we passed the ball back and forth, as much as I tried, I couldn't get my mind off of Mama.

"Did you see Bonanza last night?", I asked as I caught the ball and threw it back.

"No, I had to clean my room.", answered Jake, "Was it a good one?".

"It was alright, I guess. They kidnapped Ben's son.", I told him.

"Oh, wow, well, my mom said if you want to stay over this weekend you can.", Jake offered as we continued passing the ball.

"Yeah? That would be swell. I'll ask my old man.", I said.

"He brought home some woman. I guess to replace my mom since she's not coming back.", I said as I threw the ball a little harder, hitting Jake's mitt right in the center.

"So, she's really not coming back?", he paused before throwing the ball back to me.

"Nope, I guess he won some kind of argument. I don't know.", I reached and missed the ball as it flew above my head.

I ran over to grab it, picking it up, I turned and began walking back towards Jake.

"I think maybe she's happier without us. Seems like the old man is happier without her anyway.", I said as I tossed the ball back to Jake.

He stopped our game of catch and put the ball and mitt in the pit of his arm, "Want some seeds?", he asked as he pulled a package of sunflower seeds out of his pocket. I ran over to him and put out my hands.

We sat there on the field and waited until it was time to go back home. Spitting out seed shells in front of us, we tried spitting each one further than the last just like always.

"You spit like a girl.", I teased.

"You throw like a girl.", he teased back.

Eventually, when the sun was beginning to set, we slowly started back home.

As we got closer to our street we heard my Dad hollering, "Matthew!".

Jake and I patted the backs of our hands together and walked away from each other. I ran into the house and could smell something delicious. I was reminded of Mama and her meals she always had ready when Dad got home. Then I saw Maria in the kitchen breaking a long loaf of garlic bread that had been toasted.

Marc and Mitch were already at the table.

"Wash up, we're having a real meal tonight.", Dad said as he patted Maria on the bottom.

I went to the bathroom to wash my hands and came back to join them all at the table. Maria had made a big pot of spaghetti and meatballs. The sauce was different from how Mama had made hers. There was lots of spices and it was thicker with more tomatoes. I didn't want to admit it, but it was better than Mama's.

"Maria's going to be staying here with us.", Dad told us as he looked over at her.

She nodded her head and then said with an accent I'd never heard here in Michigan, "Yes, I am here to stay.".

"What about Mama and Daisy?", Marc asked.

I looked up at Dad to hear his answer.

He cleared his throat, "Well, they're staying at your Nanny's. But I bet you'll see them sometime.", he answered.

Dad looked over at Maria, "Maybe, I mean, if she ever calls to see you.", he added.

"Anyway, how was school?", he asked.

"It was good.", Marc answered with a mouth full of spaghetti.

"No, no.", Maria said to Marc, "No talking while you eat.".

"That's right, Marcus, where's your manners?", Dad added as he handed Marc a napkin.

Marc wiped his mouth and took a big gulp of milk, so big that it dribbled down his chin.

"Oh, you have a lot to learn.", Maria said to Marc.

We'd only known her for a few hours and she was already on my nerves, but at least she could make something better to eat than Dad's sandwiches that we'd been eating for months.

I decided I'd just try to stay quiet and out of sight the rest of the week. Maybe she wouldn't stay too long and then she'd go away.

By the weekend, she was still there. She had proven everyday what a great cook she was. Everything she made for us was some kind of Italian dish and it was ready by the time Dad got home from work each evening. She wore dresses that were different than the kind Mama wore. They flowingly hung on her and didn't show her curves as much. She didn't wear an apron when she cooked, instead, she wore a pink robe which stayed wrapped and tied around her all day. Unlike Mama, I never saw Maria wearing make-up or putting on lipstick. She mostly spoke to us boys with her big, green eyes and her finger pointing or snapping. When we got home from school she pointed outside. When we were finished with supper she pointed to our room. If she caught Mitch with his thumb in his mouth she would snap her fingers and get right in his face, almost nose to nose. In just a few days of Maria being there, she had already taught us who was in charge now.

Dad said it was okay for me to sleepover at Jake's so while he was at work I went into my room to gather a few things to take in a small blue bag. As I took the bag out of my closet I instantly thought of Mama.

"This is for when we visit Nanny. You can put anything you want to take with us in there.", she had told me when she gave it to me. I held it close to my chest for a moment and closed my eyes, trying hard to somehow feel Mama's hug through it.

I quickly wiped a tear from my eye and began packing the bag.

I packed a shirt, some jeans, my Batman comic book and as I looked around for my deck of cards, I saw a car pull up across the street through the crack between the window curtains. It was Nanny's car.

I got closer to the window and pushed the curtain a little more out of the way and saw Mama get out of the car.

"Mama.", I whispered as my heart began beating faster.

I saw her walk across the street carrying Daisy.

"Daisy.", I whispered.

I watched Maria watering the grass in the front yard and then stop to go closer to Mama. They started talking but I couldn't hear what they were saying so I moved closer to the window and pushed the curtain back a little more. Daisy looked my way and our eyes met. I put my hand up to the window as if I could touch them through it. I watched as Mama and Maria talked, Maria's hand flew through the air, waving it around as she spoke. Mama turned and walked away with Daisy still looking at me over Mama's shoulder. Maria came into the house and I could hear her shut the door behind her saying words in Italian that I didn't understand.

I continued watching Mama and Daisy as they got back into the car with Nanny and drove away.

Chapter Fifteen- (Daisy)

Weeks turned into months since Mama had spoken to the woman in the yard.

We went every weekend to visit my brothers, each time carrying the sack of teddy bears and each time leaving in disappointment when there was no answer. Mama tried calling Daddy on the phone but the woman would answer and hang up.

We had gone to Ms. Welch's office but she just told Mama to keep trying to go over there. Nanny was frustrated because Ms. Welch told her she needed more money to help. I didn't know people needed money to help you.

"I say, we go up to his work.", Nanny said one day while her and Mama were sitting on the couch folding clothes.

"I thought about that too, but what if he has us escorted out for trespassing?", Mama asked.

"Well, he may, but it's worth a shot.", Nanny answered as she put a perfectly folded shirt into a wicker basket that was on the floor next to her.

"Sometimes you've got to create a little ruckus to get yourself heard.", Nanny said as she reached for another shirt from the pile of clothes between them to fold.

"Yeah.", Mama's voice trailed off.

"I put in an application at the diner.", Mama changed the subject, "I thought I could save some money for Ms. Welch.".

"I think that's fantastic, Mable. Go out there and get your feet wet in something more than making babies.", Nanny told her as she continued folding.

Mama giggled, swatting at Nanny with a sock.

Nanny giggled too and then added, "Don't get me wrong, you do make some beautiful babies, but let's try making some biscuits and gravy now.", they both laughed.

"Looks like you and I will be spending more time together, huh, Daisy?", Nanny asked me while I reached over to grab something out of the pile of clothes to help fold. I smiled as I fluffed out a pair of my underwear, using my chest, I then folded them in half and set them in the wicker basket. Nanny was about to help me and then stopped to watch me, "Good girl, Daisy, you know what you're doing don't you?", she smiled.

"We can go to the market together everyday.", Nanny added, "You'll be a good little helper.", she said to me as she handed me another piece of clothing to fold.

Time went on and Mama started working at the diner during the day. I missed her being beside me all day, but I loved me and Nanny's adventures just as much. Nanny would load her bird cages into the backseat of the car and I would carry her smaller creations to put into the trunk. Wearing one of her lowest cut and most revealing dresses, we'd take all of it to the city market and set it out on a table there. I sat in front of a smaller table with cookies Nanny had baked to sell also.

Just before we'd start selling, we'd always make sure to put on our lipstick.

"Don't forget to smack.", she'd remind me like always.

As soon as the people would start trickling into the market Nanny would stand in front of her creations to make sure they were all in the right spot to be seen.

As people would wander through, different men would stop by and talk to Nanny about the weather or to offer her a light when she pulled out a cigarette. Some of them would just stop and stare at her, put a few dollars in the money jar that sat on the table beside the cookies I was manning and then they'd walk away. A few men even whistled at her as they walked by, but none of them ever actually talked to her about her creations she was selling. There was always the occasional woman who would stop by and marvel at the bird cages, asking her about them, most of them settling for some cookies. They'd comment on what a good little helper I was and then move on to the next booth.

When we'd go home we were usually two or three items less than what we went with and Nanny would take the money she had made out from the inside of her top. She'd sit down at the kitchen table to count it out and then stuff it into one of her hiding spots.

Mama would get in just after us from the diner. Still wearing the burgundy apron around her waist, she'd plop onto the couch with her feet sprawled out and ask us how our day went. I'd sit in her lap and tell her all about the happenings of the market from the day. Nanny would get busy making supper while Mama rested. This became our normal routine.

We had still been going over to try and see my brothers, but there was still never an answer. Each time we went Mama brought the sack of bears. Time after time, we were disappointed with no sight of the boys. After a while we both got used to the door not being answered but still held hope that one day there would be.

"I think I've got enough saved up for Ms. Welch.", Mama said after a few months of working.

"Oh, good and I've been saving too.", Nanny replied, "When do you want to go talk to her?".

"Can we go tomorrow? I'm off.", Mama answered.

Nanny nodded, "Sounds good to me. What about you, Daisy? Sound good to you?".

I nodded, not really knowing what I was agreeing to.

When we got to Ms. Welch's office the next day, she led us back to the room where her desk was. Once again, Nanny sat in the chair in front of the desk and I sat in Mama's lap in the other.

"I've been by just about every weekend.", Mama told her, "No one answers and when I call, the woman who's shacking up with him hangs up on me."

Ms. Welch wrote down what Mama was saying and then looked up at her, "Okay, so what we can do now is get a judge to sign off on an officer to go with you."

"Okay, but what if he still doesn't answer?", Nanny asked.

"Well, then we'll go from there.", Ms. Welch assured them, "In the meantime, I'll get the judge's signature and I'll call Mr. Thompson. ".

Mama and Nanny both took out money from their purses. Nanny handed over a few different bills and Mama had a tall stack of dollar bills all folded together. They put the money on the desk and Ms. Welch picked it up and began counting it all.

As she went through the dollar bills Mama looked down in embarrassment, "I'm sorry. It's all my tip money.", she said.

"Money's money.", Ms. Welch shrugged.

"That's exactly what I told her.", Nanny said matter of factly.

When she finished counting the money, Ms. Welch opened a drawer in her desk and pulled out a white envelope. Stuffing the neatly stacked money into the envelope she said, "Okay, I'll let you know when I have the judge's order."

A few days went by when Mama got home from the diner, coming in excitedly, "She got it! She got the judge's order!".

She nearly danced her way in through the house, "We'll go this weekend."

Nanny ran out from the kitchen and hugged Mama, "Oh, that's wonderful!", she cried out.

"Since there's an officer coming with me, it might be best to leave Daisy behind this time.", she looked over at me, "We just don't know how he'll react to that."

"I completely agree. I'll stay here with her while you go.", Nanny smiled and then went to start supper, "Oh, finally! I'm just so happy right now!".

That weekend Mama went, once again, with the sack of teddy bears to try and see the boys. She kissed me on the head and hugged Nanny before she left. Her excitement brought on nervousness. She had changed her dress three times and then wandered around for about thirty minutes looking for her keys that were on the kitchen table.

"Okay, here goes nothing.", she looked back at us, taking in a deep breath and then blowing it out as she finally walked out the door.

"Hold your head high, baby!", Nanny hollered just before Mama closed the door.

"Well, there she goes.", Nanny said to me.

"Nanny?", I began to ask a question.

"Yes, baby girl?", Nanny reached over and pushed the hair out of my eyes.

"Why doesn't Daddy like me?", I looked down into my lap as I asked.

"Oh, honey.", she took me in her arms and held me in her lap on the couch. Sitting there together, she thought for a moment before she answered. "Now, you listen to me.", turning me around in her lap, she tipped my chin up with her finger and then put her hands on my shoulders.

"You are beautiful and funny and ohhh so smart. Don't you give anyone who don't agree a second thought.", she looked into my eyes as she spoke, "There's not one reason I can think of that would make someone not like you. Seems to me they must not like themselves too much.", she grinned and then hugged me again.

"Now, how about we go make some brownies?", she gave me a tight squeeze, "Or I could just go ahead and eat you up!", she pretended to bite my neck which tickled, making me laugh hysterically.

"No, Nanny! Don't eat me!", I pushed through my laughs.

"Well, then we'd better get to it!", she picked me up and carried me into the kitchen.

Nanny and I mixed and stirred as we talked about her next ideas of creations to make. She asked me what I thought about her making some vases with some of the bottles she had collected and ashtrays made out of bottle caps and tuna cans. I loved hearing all about her ideas and her plans on how to make them happen.

Just as we were about to put the brownies into the oven we heard Mama pull up in front of the house.

"Is that your Mama already?", Nanny was puzzled as she closed the oven door.

When Mama came inside, Nanny looked at her with her hands on her hips, "That was quick. You're back already?", she asked, confused.

Mama carried the sack of teddy bears and set it on the table. She slowly pulled out a chair at the table and sat down. Not speaking a word she set her purse on the floor and stared out the window looking as if she'd seen a ghost.

"Well, what happened?", Nanny walked over beside her.

Mama continued staring out the window and then slowly began to speak, "The officer met me there...no one was there...I knocked but...no one was there.", her bottom lip began to quiver as she spoke and tears began rolling down her cheeks.

"So will the officer go back with you again?", Nanny asked.

Mama looked up at Nanny, "No...no one was there. Nothing was there.".

"What do you mean nothing was there?", Nanny shook her head trying to understand and then sat down across from Mama.

Mama's tears continued to roll down her face as she kept her eyes on Nanny, "The house was empty.", she said, "They're gone.".

Chapter Sixteen- (Matt)

At Jake's house I decided not to talk about anything that was going on at home. It was nice to be away from Maria and I just wanted to think about anything but her. We spent our time looking through my comic book and sorting out Jake's baseball card collection. We lined them all up, each player's card with their team. He had all the greats, Mays, Mantle and Aaron were a few of my favorites. We argued over who was the best and then settled on our favorite legend, Babe.

I hoped that when I came back home Maria would be gone, however, when I got back from my sleepover, there was no such luck. As soon as I walked back in the house, she was in the kitchen talking on the phone. She hardly looked at me as she pointed to the backyard where she wanted me to go. I sat my bag down and went outside to find Marc and Mitch digging in the dirt with some old gardening shovels. I sat on the back porch and began thinking about how long it would take to dig a hole to China. I imagined finally breaking through the ground on the other side of the world, sweaty and dirty, to find faces that didn't look like mine. They would help me crawl out of the hole and pat me on the back and then carry me on their shoulders as if I were some sort of hero as they cheered in a language I couldn't understand.

The cloud of imagination vanished as I wondered about Mama and Daisy after seeing them through the window. I thought about how I should have ran out to her or at least tapped on the window to get her attention. I kept remembering her look of disappointment as she turned to walk away with Daisy's face over her shoulder.

As time went on from that day, we became busier on the weekends. Running errands, visiting our Uncle Joe, Dad's older brother, or sometimes going to the lake to fish. Occasionally, Aunt Becky would come along with us. When she was with us Maria seemed to act a little differently. She was somewhat kinder.

One time Aunt Becky joined us at Dad's favorite fishing hole. Marc was trying his best to squeeze a worm onto his hook when Maria walked over to see him struggling.

"Let me help.", Maria said to him as she took the worm he was holding and poked the hook into it. Marc cast the line into the water and looked at Maria for approval. As they stood there with their poles by the water, Dad was busy helping Mitch learn how to cast his line. I didn't like fishing. It was boring. So, I spent most of my time throwing rocks into the pond trying to make them skip on the water.

"Here, like this.", Aunt Becky instructed as she picked up a rock and tossed it sideways. It gently went bouncing across the water and then disappeared.

"How'd you do that?", I said in amazement after what felt like a thousand attempts of me tossing rock after rock. She giggled at me and then looked over her shoulder at Maria and Marc still holding their poles.

"How are you doing, kid?", she asked in a whisper.

I looked up at her unsure of what she wanted to know about, "I'm okay.", was all I could come up with. Maria noticed us standing off to the side and walked over towards us, clapping her hands, "Ready to eat?", she asked as she tapped Aunt Becky on the shoulder.

"Sure.", Aunt Becky answered and then patted me on the back, "Come on, I'm starving.".

Over time, it became very clear that Maria did not like Mama. When Mitch or Marc would mention Mama, Maria would narrow her eyes at them and tell them to forget about her or ask them why they were talking about someone who doesn't care about them.

When they mentioned anything about Daisy, she would laugh and call her the bastard child who doesn't even know her father.

I quickly figured out that keeping quiet about Mama and Daisy kept me in somewhat of good standings with Maria. She expected more out of me than Mama did as far as chores went. I washed the dishes every night, made sure my brothers did their homework and took baths, I hung the clothes on the line and then folded them every weekend. When there was cleaning to be done, I jumped to it, quickly sweeping or picking up things around the house in order to stay out of trouble.

One evening, while Dad was in the shower, Marc decided to challenge her when she told him to clean off the table. After supper, I had begun my routine of washing dishes when I heard him in the living room begin to argue about cleaning the table.

"But I don't want to.", he said in a whiney voice, "I'm playing trucks.".

I heard her jump up off the couch and stomp across the room to him, snapping her fingers, "Little boy! You will do what I say!", she yelled at him.

He began crying, again saying, "I don't want to.", over and over.

She snatched him up by the collar of his shirt and dragged him into the kitchen beside the table. Swatting his behind as he stumbled to keep up with her, he tried to block her swats with his hands covering his bottom.

As she held onto his shirt, she pulled him around with her to the sink where I was standing. Nudging me out of her way, she flung open the cabinet doors under the sink and took out a rag. She held the rag under the water that was still running in the sink, squeezed it out and shoved it into Marc's hand. He took the rag and threw it on the floor.

She picked him up off the floor by his shirt and threw him over the chair.

Hitting him again and again all over, wherever her hand landed on his body as he twisted and turned, still crying, "No! I don't want to!".

She picked up the rag, swooped him up out of the chair and grabbed his hand. Then, she shoved the rag back into his hand and squeezed it tightly into hers. With the rag clutched in his hand with hers, she began wiping the table aggressively, with each stroke banging his body into the table.

"Ow! You're hurting me!", he hollered as she angrily wiped the table with the rag in his hand.

"You will obey me!", she yelled back at him.

When she had wiped only half of the table, she took the rag and threw it on the table.

"Now, go!", she threw him down on the ground and pointed to the bedroom as he continued crying. He looked up at her as she yelled again, "Go!", raising her hand to hit him. He covered his head with his hands and quickly scampered off to the bedroom, crying all the way.

Mitch was sitting on the living room floor beside some toy trucks as he silently watched, thumb in his mouth. I stood there beside the sink, frozen, not making a sound. She watched him run off and then turned back to the table and grabbed the rag to finish wiping the table. She looked at me and snapped, "Get finished!".

I got back to the dishes I was washing, hurrying to get them done.

When Maria finished wiping the table she went back into the living area, snapped her fingers in front of Mitch's face and sat on the couch. Mitch immediately took his thumb out of his mouth when she snapped. Letting out a sigh, she spoke under her breath in Italian and picked up a magazine that was sitting on the end table next to her. I finished the dishes in record time and as she flipped through the magazine I went to the bedroom to check on Marc. Mitch followed behind me as I went into the room where I found Marc laying in the bed still crying. I felt bad for him so I laid down next to him. Mitch crawled up into the bed and squeezed in next to me. Putting his thumb back into his mouth, the three of us laid there side by side and stared at the ceiling with only the sound of Marc's whimpers.

Mama would have never hit us like that I thought.

The next morning while we got ready for school, Marc was on the floor of our bedroom putting on his shoes when Dad came in.

He patted me lightly on the head as I buttoned my shirt. Then, he reached down and slapped the back of Marc's head, "When Maria tells you to do something, you do it, boy.". He spoke very calmly as Marc quickly reached up to grab his head and let out a shout in surprise.

Dad walked out of the room as Marc looked up at me, rubbing his head with angry tears in his eyes. Rubbing his eyes he began tying his shoes.

There was no breakfast waiting for us that morning before we left for school and as Jake met up with us while we walked, none of us spoke.

"Why's everyone so quiet?", he asked.

I looked over at him and punched him in the shoulder.

He grabbed his shoulder, "Ow, what did I do?".

Avoiding his question, I walked faster, getting ahead of him and my brothers. Nothing else was said as we continued our walk.

That evening when we were back at home starting the nightly routine of me washing dishes, Marc came into the kitchen and reached under the sink for a rag. He quietly began wiping the table when Maria walked up behind him. She stood with her hands on her hips and then crossed her arms, she nodded with a pleased look on her face. The two of us worked silently through our chores as she watched over us.

At supper, Dad and Maria talked about a place in New Mexico. Nothing much was said about it but I got the feeling maybe they were planning to take a trip there when Dad said, "I've got all that we'll need taken care of for it.".

Later, while we were laying in bed, I heard Dad and Maria talking.

"She's trying to destroy us.", he said, "Mr. Thompson told me today that she's bringing an officer over here this weekend.".

I listened as closely as I could.

"Have you heard anything from Joe about the job?", she asked.

"He's working on it for me and as soon as he says so, we'll head that way.".

Uncle Joe was Dad's older brother who was different from Dad. I never saw him without a smile and his belly shook when he laughed. Shorter than Dad, he had light brown hair and deep set brown eyes. Uncle Joe always seemed to be in a good mood.

We would go to his house some evenings where the adults would play cards while the kids played. Aunt Becky usually came too and always made sure to visit with us kids before going to play with the adults. Uncle Joe's wife, Aunt Bess, was sweet and quiet. She laughed at all of Uncle Joe's jokes and seemed to enjoy everyone around the table playing cards. Before, when Mama was there, they would sit beside each other and have quiet side conversations while the men told big, loud stories. But, when Maria started coming, replacing Mama's seat at the card table, Aunt Bess didn't speak much to her. Maria was loud and sarcastic. She was there to play cards and she was really good so she came to win.

"Well Maria, you got me again.", Uncle Joe would say at the end of a round as he showed her his cards. Maria would laugh loudly and start shuffling the cards to play again. Aunt Bess seemed annoyed with Maria and would most of the time leave the game to come join us in our cousin's room. She'd quietly sit in the corner and knit while she watched us play. Our two cousins, Steve and Jane, were older than me by a few years. Steve was a master at checkers and would play with me while Marc and Mitch played with Steve's old toys. Now that Daisy wasn't with us, Jane would mostly stay in her own room. Daisy loved Jane, she was like a big sister to her. Together, they played with dolls and make-up and Daisy followed Jane around, mimicking everything she did.

I could tell that our visits now without Daisy or Mama weren't as pleasant for Aunt Bess or Jane, but they both still acted happy to see us boys when we showed up.

The last time we were there, Uncle Joe patted Dad on the shoulder as we were leaving, "It shouldn't be long before I hear something. I'll let you know.", he told Dad.

I didn't know what he was talking about then, but now listening in on Dad and Maria's conversation, I realized Uncle Joe was helping Dad get a job somewhere. Dad had worked at the plastic factory my whole life. I had no idea he was planning on leaving it.

I laid there hoping they would give more information while they talked, but they went to their bedroom where I couldn't hear them anymore.

Who's trying to destroy us?, I wondered, And how? Why are they bringing an officer? And what about New Mexico? Are they taking us with them?

Trying to make sense of it all, I fell asleep.

The next night, I was awoken by Dad coming into our bedroom quietly. In the darkness, he began opening our dresser drawers and pulling out all of our clothes, stuffing them into a garbage bag. I sat straight up in my bed, rubbing my eyes, I whispered, "Dad?".

He stopped what he was doing for a moment and looked over at me, "Put your shoes on.", he whispered back. I pushed the blanket off of me and got out of bed, confused as he tossed my shoes over to me.

He tied a knot in the top of the garbage bag full of clothes and then stepped out of the room with it over his shoulder. Maria was walking back and forth down the hallway, carrying boxes and bags as she went in and out of the house.

I quickly put my shoes on, wondering what was going on but too afraid to ask. Dad appeared back in the bedroom, looking around he grabbed my blue bag that Mama had given me and handed it to me, "Put whatever you want to take in here.", still whispering. He stepped back out of the room and started helping Maria carry things out to the car. I grabbed my comic books, the GI Joes, my deck of cards and anything else that I saw and put it in the blue bag.

"Ready?", I heard Dad ask Maria as he walked back into the bedroom.

"You got everything?", he asked me. I nodded my head, wondering if I was dreaming.

He reached into the bed where Marc and Mitch were still sleeping. Sliding his arms under Mitch, he pulled him up out of bed, wrapped him with a blanket and carried him out of the room.

"Come on.", he said to me as he walked out.

I looked back at my room as I walked out behind him and followed him to the car still in my pajamas. He put Mitch in the backseat of the station wagon, adjusting the blanket around him.

"I'll go get Marc and then we're off.", he told Maria as she got into the front seat. Before getting in, I noticed a trailer connected to the back of the car with most of our belongings. The back of the station wagon was filled to the roof, overflowing with things above the top of the backseat. I got in the backseat next to Mitch who was now looking around groggy. He put his head on my shoulder and fell back to sleep, unphased as to why we were in the car in the middle of the night. Dad came out of the house holding Marc in his arms and closed the door behind him. He put him in the backseat next to Mitch and threw a blanket over him. Marc curled up next to the other side of Mitch as Dad got in the car.

He looked over at Maria, "I think we got everything.", he said to her. Maria nodded and we drove away under a moonlit night sky.

Chapter Seventeen- (Daisy)

"I went over there with the officer. Everything is gone. They just up and moved.", Mama told Ms. Welch on the phone.

She paced back and forth in the kitchen as she talked, carrying the yellow, bell shaped dial box in her hand, the cord dragged along across the floor with her movements.

Nanny paced behind her in a circle, smoking one cigarette after another.

"Okay. Uh huh.", Mama said, "Yes, he has a brother, Joe Mair.", she told Ms. Welch, "Okay, I'll let you know. Okay.", she put the receiver on the phone and sat it back on the counter.

"Well?", Nanny asked.

"She said we should go to his work and ask him where he moved. We can talk to Joe too, if that doesn't work out.", Mama answered.

"Well, then, let's go.", Nanny said as she grabbed her purse and walked to the front door. Mama picked me up from where I was standing and rushed out the door behind Nanny, neither of them worried about lipstick.

We pulled into the parking lot of the plastic factory. Nanny drove up and down the rows of cars.

"I don't see his car.", Mama said as she looked around at all of the parked cars.

"I don't either.", Nanny agreed as she parked.

115

We got out of the car and walked up to the entrance of the factory. Mama held my hand with Nanny walking right beside her. When we went inside, a musty smell welcomed us at the door. There were two big desks at the front with rows and rows of filing cabinets behind them. There was a large picture window next to the desks with a glass door that led into the factory. Through the window I could see large machines with conveyor belts, all moving sheets of plastic. Men with white hard hats walked around, some pushing buttons on the machines, some carrying sheets of plastic.

A man in a blue collared, button up shirt with a name tag, the same kind I'd seen Daddy wear, noticed us. He walked through the door from the factory and into the entrance where we were standing.

He took off the hard hat he was wearing, "Hello ladies, what can I do for you?", he asked.

"We need to speak with Mike Mair.", Mama told him.

Scratching his head, the man said, "Oh, Mike? He's not with us anymore.".

Mama's jaw dropped wide open and then softly she asked, "What do you mean?".

"Well, ma'am, Mike quit a few days ago.", he answered.

Mama turned to look at Nanny who asked, "Do you know where he went?".

"No, ma'am. All I know is he got a job somewhere else.", the man told her, "Can I do anything else for you?".

"No, sir. Thank you, that's all we needed.", Nanny answered as she grabbed Mama by the elbow and led her out the front door still holding my hand.

We got back in the car, Nanny slamming her door behind us.

"That son of a...", she paused as she looked over at me and then Mama.

"What has he done?", Nanny said sternly as she pulled out of the parking lot.

Mama stared out the window and began twirling her hair with her finger.

"Let's go talk to Joe.", Nanny said.

I hadn't seen Uncle Joe and Aunt Bess in a long time. I always had fun playing with my cousin, Jane, when we'd go over for the adults to play cards. We'd play with her Barbies, something I didn't have of my own. She had so many of them, she kept them in a big pink case with all of their clothes. There was an outfit for every season for each doll.

When we got to their house, Nanny parked in the curved driveway in front of the house. They had a big, nice house made of bricks and big black stones. It had lots of windows all around and a long front porch. The inside was just as big and pretty as the outside, always spotless with everything in order.

The three of us got out of the car and walked up to the front door. I couldn't wait to see Jane and thought maybe I'd get a little time to play with her and the Barbies.

When Uncle Joe answered the door, he had a big smile when he saw us, "Oh, hello, Mable.", he reached his arms out to give her a hug.

He put his hand out to shake Nanny's, still smiling he said, "Hi Peggy. It's good to see you.".

"Oh, and look at that, you brought the munchkin.", he laughed as he reached down to poke my belly.

"How are you girls doing? I haven't seen you in ages.", he asked as we stood on the porch.

"Well, we're looking for Mike and the boys. Have you seen them?", Mama asked.

"Oh, yeah, I saw them not too long ago", he replied, "Didn't he tell you about the new job I got him?", he put his hand in his pocket and started jingling change. He pulled out a handful of the change and held it in the palm of his hand. Using his finger, he scooted the coins around in his hand as if he were counting them. Then, he took four quarters and handed them to me, "Here, baby girl, now you go buy something good with that.", he smiled and winked at me.

"What new job?", Mama asked, puzzled.

"Oh, you know, the one down in New Mexico. Working at a parts warehouse.", he told her as he pointed his thumb behind him.

"What? Did you say New Mexico?", Nanny interrupted in nearly a shout.

"Well, now, Mabel, I thought he told you all about it. He said you were fine with it.", he said as he started to look concerned.

"Now, why in the world would I be fine with him taking my babies six states away?", Mama asked with her arms crossed.

"Well, I wondered that myself, to be honest.", Uncle Joe answered as his smile began to fade away.

"Did he tell you we haven't seen or heard from him or the boys in months?", Nanny asked snidely.

Uncle Joe cleared his throat, "Is that right?", he crossed his arms, "Peggy, I really had no idea that you two didn't know all this.", his smile completely gone now.

"Well you're not the only one in the dark.", Nanny said.

"I need to sit down.", Mama said as she sat down on the top step of the porch. She put her head in her hands and spoke slowly, "Joe, please, just tell me everything you know.".

Uncle Joe sat down next to Mama on the step as Nanny pulled a cigarette out of her purse.

"Mabel, I'm sorry. This is all my fault.", he said as he looked at his feet.

"What do you mean it's all your fault?", Nanny asked as she paced in front of them on the concrete path that led to the porch.

"I mentioned to him one time when he was here with that Italian woman...", he paused, "You do know about her, right?", looking up at Nanny.

Mama nodded her head.

"I don't know what he sees in her.", he shuddered.

"Anyway, I mentioned to Mike that I had a buddy who was having trouble with his warehouse down there and didn't have enough men to work.", Uncle Joe rubbed his forehead.

"I didn't mean nothing by it, really. But he kept pestering me about it and told me he had talked to you. He said you two had it all worked out, so I gave him my buddy's name and number.", he blew a big breath out of his mouth.

"Do you know when he left?", Mama asked.

"As far as I know, they were leaving over the weekend.", he answered.

"Could you give us the name and number of your friend?", Nanny asked as she put out her cigarette on the concrete.

"Oh, sure, of course. I'll help you however I can.", he said as he stood back up and then helped Mama stand.

"I'll be right back.", he stepped into the house.

Mama and Nanny stared at each other, amazed at what they'd just learned.

Uncle Joe came back with a little piece of paper and handed it to Mama, "There you go. I hope that helps.".

Mama reached to give him a hug, "Thanks, Joe. I really do appreciate it.", she told him.

"Oh, Mabel, you've always been special to me. He never did treat you right.", he told her, "Now, don't be a stranger.".

Nanny stepped up and shook Uncle Joe's hand, "Thank you, Joe. I always knew she ended up with the wrong brother.".

When we got back home, both Nanny and Mama threw their purses on the ground and kicked off their shoes.

They plopped down on the couch and I sat in between them. Mama ran her fingers through my hair and began to cry. Nanny said nothing as she sat there with her legs curled up underneath her, staring into space. The feelings of defeat and devastation surrounded us as we sat there in silence.

I didn't completely understand what this was all about but I knew it was terribly sad, so I curled up in Mama's arms and let the comfort of being close to her soothe me. The three of us stayed there on the couch until evening became night. And as the moon and stars showed through the blinds we fell asleep in a small pile trying, somehow, to find strength in each other and some sort of peace in the stillness.

Chapter Eighteen- (Matt)

We drove through the night and the next day, stopping once on the side of the road for Dad to sleep. At one point, Marc asked where we were going and Dad told him we were going to a new house.

I didn't understand what was going on, so when Dad mentioned a new house I began to feel sad and angry all at the same time.

A new house?, I thought, Where? What about Mama and Daisy? Will I ever see them again?.

Then I thought about Jake, I didn't even get to say goodbye.

We stopped at a few gas stations along the way and then at a rest stop where Dad made us bologna sandwiches and took a nap in the car.

Marc and Mitch got restless in the backseat and began making blowing noises with their mouths on their arms. When they began getting louder and started laughing, Maria looked back at them and snapped her fingers for them to stop.

I started a game with them looking for Volkswagen Beetles. Everytime we saw one we'd punch each other in the arm, "Slug-Bug!", we'd holler. The more I found, the harder I punched, eventually ending the game with Mitch crying and Dad telling us that was enough.

When we finally got closer to where we were going, after a drive that I thought would be endless, I knew this was it when Dad said, "Here we are. The Land of Enchantment.". I didn't know what that meant but it sounded like it had to be something good.

When we arrived in a dead looking town, we turned down some dusty roads and then pulled into a driveway in front of a peach colored Adobe house. It was getting dark when we got out of the car. Dad got out and walked up to the house, "Stay here.", he said.

We waited by the car as he went inside the house. I looked around to see mostly dirt and rocks, no trees like I was used to seeing in Michigan. Lined down the street were more Adobe houses, something I'd only ever seen in books at school when we talked about the Indians.

Dad came out, grinning and rubbing his hands together, "It's just like he said. Everything we need.", he told Maria.

He went to the trailer and started unloading boxes, "Matthew, Marcus, go grab something.", he told us as he walked past us and back into the house. Me and Marc went around to the trailer and each grabbed a box, light enough for us to carry.

"Grab the blankets, Mitchie.", I ordered.

Maria took a box and went into the house behind us. The house smelled like dust and had cracks up and down the walls.

"Home, sweet, home.", Dad said as he flicked on the lights in the living area.

Nothing about this home felt sweet to me. There was an old brown sofa in the living room with a few small rips in the seat cushions which showed the white stuffing inside.

"There's a room for you, Matt, all to yourself. Marc and Mitch, you can share the other one.", Dad waved for us to follow him down the dimly lit hallway. He pointed to the first bedroom, "Matt.", he said as he kept walking. He stopped in front of the next bedroom that had another one across the hall from it, "Marc. Mitch.", he said as he pointed.

I'd never had my own bedroom before. I had always shared with my brothers.

Maria came up behind us and went into the bedroom for her and Dad. Each bedroom had a bed and a dresser for our clothes.

I went into my new bedroom and sat on the bed, "Home, sweet, home.", I whispered as I looked around.

We settled in quickly over the next few days, unpacking boxes and hanging things on the walls. Dad made sure there was a place for everything and showed us where everything should be put away. Maria got acquainted with the stove in the kitchen, quickly getting back to cooking her Italian dishes.

"Tomorrow, I'll take you over to the school.", Dad said as we sat at the table for supper one evening. Marc picked at his plate full of pasta, "Do we have to go to school?", he whined.

Dad chuckled, "Of course you do, boy. I'll be starting work tomorrow too.", Dad answered.

Maria slapped her hand on the table in front of Marc, making him and his plate jump, "Quit playing with it and eat it.", she said through her teeth.

"I don't want to.", he whined.

"Eat it.", she snarled.

Dad got up from the table to take his plate to the sink and then went to get in the bath since this house didn't have a shower, on his way telling Marc, "Marcus, do what you're told.".

Marc slid down in his chair and pouted with his arms crossed in front of him. Maria reached over and pulled him up by his shirt, "I said eat.".

She took the fork on his plate and stabbed it into a noodle. Then, she put the noodle up to his face and shoved it in his mouth as she squeezed his cheeks with her other hand. Marc started to cry as she began shoving noodle after noodle into his mouth. He started gagging and coughing as he wasn't able to keep up with the noodles being forced into his mouth all at once.

Watching in fear for him, I stood up and yelled at her, "Stop it!".

She stopped and turned to look at me, putting the fork down, she reached over and slapped my cheek, "Don't tell me what to do, young man.", she gritted her teeth as I rubbed my cheek. Marc coughed and cried, spitting out noodles and chewing what was left in his mouth.

"Go! All of you!", she pointed towards our bedrooms.

"But I'm still hungry.", Mitch cried.

She stood up from the table and took Mitch's plate out from under him and then grabbed mine and Marc's, "Go, I said!", she glared at us.

"I hate you! I want Mama back!", I yelled as I stomped off to my room with Marc and Mitch following behind me.

Instead of going to their room, they came into mine. I pounded the bed with my fists as hard as I could and then reached over to pick up my pillow to throw it across the room almost hitting Mitch.

"Hey!", he screeched and then put his thumb in his mouth.

I sat on my bed with my elbows on my knees. Marc sat down next to me and Mitch sat on the other side of me, thumb still in his mouth.

I put my arm around Marc's shoulder, "You ok?", I asked. Marc grabbed his mouth, "Yeah.".

Taking his thumb out of his mouth, Mitch asked, "Matt? What happened to Mama and Daisy?".

"I don't really know. I think Mama left us.", I answered unsure of what to say.

"Why?", Marc asked next.

"I don't know.", getting frustrated by their questions, "Would you two quit asking all the questions?".

I crawled around Marc and laid down on the bed.

"Matt?", Mitch asked.

"What?", I sighed.

"Can we sleep with you tonight?", he asked, popping his thumb out of his mouth to talk and then putting it right back.

I scooted over to give them room to lay down beside me.

Mitch wrapped his arms and legs around me and Marc laid close to the edge of the bed. I'm not sure, but I think we were all thinking about the same thing, Mama.

The next day, Dad had gotten up early to get ready for work. He woke the three of us, still sleeping in my bed together, "Can't get you guys to separate, can I?", he said.

I was relieved to know that Maria was still in bed when we left to go to our new school. She was the last person I wanted to see that morning.

On the way to school, Mitch asked Dad something none of us had asked in a while, "Daddy, where is Mama and Daisy?".

Dad glanced back at him in the backseat as he drove, "Well, Mitchie, she just didn't want to be with us anymore.".

Marc piped in, "But why?".

Dad shrugged his shoulders, "She went to go be with Daisy's father. She never cared about us.".

I spoke up, "But, you are Daisy's father.".

Looking over at me he said, "Nope, she is a bastard. I only make boys.".

Then, as we all got quiet, he finished the conversation with, "The best thing you boys can do is to forget about them. Your Mama has moved on and so should you.".

When we got to the school, it was a small, red bricked building. We went inside where Dad introduced us to the principal, "Matthew, Marcus and Mitchell.", he pointed to each of us.

The principal smiled and began to lead us down a long hallway as Dad left.

He showed Marc and Mitch to their classrooms and then walked with me to mine. I was nervous about being in a new school, especially since I'd only ever gone to one.

As we got to my classroom door, the principal opened it and walked in. A teacher was in the front of the class, writing on the chalkboard as I followed the principal inside.

"Class...", he interrupted. There were rows of kids sitting at desks, holding books. They all put their books down and the teacher stopped writing to look over at us.

Once he had everyone's attention, the principal went on, "This is Matthew Mair. Let's all show him some kindness today as he joins us.".

Everyone was staring at me, which made me want to turn and run. I put my head down, looking at my feet.

The teacher walked over to me, "Hello, Matthew, it's nice to meet you.", she said, "Let's get you a seat and a book.".

The principal left and as the teacher walked me to an empty desk in the back of the class, I felt everyone's eyes on me, like lasers.

I sat down at the desk, never looking up until the teacher handed me a book, "There you go. We're on page forty-eight.", she said as she turned to walk back to the front.

She reminded me of Mama with her dark curled hair just above her shoulders, her soft voice and her long legs under her green dress, the kind Mama wore. As awkward as it felt with all the kids staring at me and whispering to each other, something about this teacher calmed my nerves.

I looked around at the other kids who looked different than the kids at my school in Michigan.

Most of them had tan or light brown skin and black hair. I realized I was the only blonde kid in the classroom and I felt immediately out of place. I was used to being the only blonde but not the only one with my skin color. Maybe Dad brought me to the wrong school., I thought.

I tried to act like the kids staring at me didn't bother me. When we went to lunch, I sat across from two boys who kept whispering and I was sure it was about me.

At our outside break, I sat by myself under a tree by a chain linked fence. I watched the other kids play in a dirt field with a soccer ball and others swung on a long set of swings. They spoke to each other in a language I didn't know and had never heard in Michigan except for some old Westerns I'd seen with Nanny. Even then, I still understood what was being said but here, I didn't. There were some girls on a patch of concrete skipping rope and playing hopscotch. I picked at what dry grass I could find under me. I wondered about what Jake was doing and if he was mad at me for not telling him goodbye.

As I sat there alone, a group of boys came walking up to me.

"Hey. What's your name?", one of them asked.

They stood around staring at me like I was some kind of new species.

I stood up, poked out my chest and spoke confidently, "Who wants to know?".

They all took a step backwards, "Damn, gringo, we're not trying to fight.".

The whistle blew and everyone went running into the school. I walked slowly behind everyone and went back inside.

I got through the rest of the day and waited after school outside, beside the flagpole for the bus, where Marc and Mitch met up with me.

"I don't like this school.", I said to them as we waited.

"It's not that bad.", Marc waved at a boy walking past us who waved back.

"See you tomorrow, Marc.", the boy said.

"That's my new friend.", Marc told me and Mitch, "His name is Jose".

Riding the bus was a new experience for us. We had always walked to and from school so when we got on and started walking down the rows of bench seats full of kids we had a hard time pushing through legs and arms that flew by us from them kicking and hitting each other, jumping from seat to seat. We found an empty row near the back and scooted in close to each other. A boy in front of us turned around and stared over his seat at us.

"What are you staring at, prick?", I said to him with my fist held up. He quickly turned back around in his seat after showing him who's boss.

When the bus dropped us off at home, we could smell Maria's cooking from outside the house. Dad was just getting home too, "Hey, boys.", he said as we all walked in together.

"Ciao", Maria said to us as we all went to wash up for supper.

She stood beside the table just as she always did, waiting for us to come back from the bathroom and show her our hands. If they were clean enough for her, she would point to the table and if not, she slapped our hands and pointed to the sink.

Once we were all sitting, Dad asked, "How was school?".

"Good.", I replied and began eating.

"My teacher is really nice.", Mitch said as he stuffed a piece of sausage in his mouth.

Marc never spoke, he ate very slowly, trying not to make it obvious that he was scooting his food to one side of his plate. Finally, we had an evening where everyone ate in peace when the phone rang.

Dad got up from the table to answer it, "Oh, hello, Joe.". He stood against the counter where the phone sat, "I did tell her...Yes...I don't know why she said that.", he told Uncle Joe, "Let me sort this out and I'll get back to you.".

He hung up the phone, looked at Maria and then sat back down to finish eating.

Chapter Nineteen- (Daisy)

Mama called the number that Uncle Joe had given her everyday when she got home from the diner, but never got an answer so she stopped after a few weeks of trying.

She had visited with Ms. Welch who sent her to the police station.

The policeman she talked to told her that since the custody papers didn't define the visitation and Daddy was the legal guardian, there was nothing they could do for her.

Mama continued painting in the shed on most of her days off and eventually, she had so many paintings she decided to let Nanny take them to the market.

"Whatever I make from them, I can add to the tips I've been saving and then we can go down to New Mexico.", she told Nanny one evening.

"I think that's a wonderful idea, Mabel.", Nanny told her.

Mama had also tried talking to Uncle Joe again, but he told her he still didn't know much.

"Of course he's going to cover for him.", Nanny said, "He's his brother. What can he do?".

"I know.", Mama agreed, "Why does this have to be so hard?", she asked.

"I don't know, honey, but the best thing you can do is to just keep getting up and swinging, even when you're bruised and bloodied.", Nanny told her, "Keep fighting the battle.".

So much time went by, weeks turned into months and then those turned into a couple of years. Mama kept the teddy bears in the brown paper sack in the closet, still waiting to be given to the boys. Sometimes, she sat with a picture of the three of them and talked to them as if they were really there. Mama also picked up smoking more, it became an everyday habit. She lit up a new cigarette just as soon as she put one out.

I eventually started school and learned how to navigate in the world as an only child, telling anyone who asked that I didn't have any brothers or sisters.

Over time, I didn't ask about the boys anymore, in fact, I slowly began to forget about them all together. I started to forget what Daddy looked like and how he sounded.

Then, one day, Mama came home from the diner and brought in the mail. She held up a white envelope and threw the rest on the table.

"Mom! Look!", she cried out as she held the envelope up to show Nanny.

Nanny walked up closer to Mama, "What is it?", she asked.

"I don't know, but look who it's from.", she said as tears filled her wide eyes.

Nanny looked closer at the envelope and then at Mama, "Well open it up and read it already!", Nanny said excitedly as she clasped her hands together.

I joined them at the table as they both sat down, "What is it, Mama?", I curiously asked.

She looked over at me, smiled and began opening the envelope. As she unfolded the white piece of paper that was inside, Nanny patted the table impatiently, "Well, go on, read it.", she said.

Nanny and I listened intently with our eyes glued to Mama as she read, " Dear Mama...", her eyes filled with tears again as she put her hand to her chest. She took a deep breath and kept reading, "I don't know if you will remember me. I had to write someone special for school. So I wrote you. I am in fifth grade now. Marc is in third grade and Mitchie is in second grade.", tears rolled down Mama's cheeks as she read, "I miss you. I don't know if you will get this letter. I live in New Mexico. It is hot here. Not cold like Michigan. Tell Nanny and Daisy hi. I miss them. I love you. Your son, Matthew Mair.", Mama held the paper to her chest and let out a loud cry. Nanny reached over to grab her hand as she cried too.

Mama looked at the paper, reading it to herself again, she gently touched the words with her finger.

"Why did they go to New Mexico?", I asked both of them as they continued crying. Neither of them answered as Nanny got up to get some tissues.

Nanny sat back down, wiping her eyes with the tissue and handing some to Mama.

"They still think about me.", Mama said.

"Well, of course they do. You're their Mama. You never forget your Mama.", Nanny told her.

"You should try calling that number Joe gave you again.", Nanny suggested.

Mama put her finger on her chin as she thought, "Yes, I'll do that. It's been so long since I've tried. Maybe they'll answer now.".

I picked up the envelope that the letter was delivered in and held it in front of me. The writing was a little hard to read, but I could see Matt's name at the top and Mama's name in the middle of the envelope. Instantly, memories of my brothers filled my head. I remembered us playing hide and seek, "One, two, three...", I remembered Matt counting as I ran to hide in the closet of my bedroom. I'd hide and listen for him to stop counting, then get excited when I could hear him coming to look for us. When he'd make it into my room, he could hear me giggling which always helped him find me first. I remembered him opening the closet to find me sitting there, "I got you!", he'd holler as he tickled me and I would laugh hysterically. Then he'd put his finger to his lips and say, "Okay, now let's go find Marc and Mitch.". I'd excitedly follow him to roam around the house looking for them.

The next day, Mama called the number and to her surprise, someone answered. She told Nanny it was some man who knew Daddy. The man took her name and number and told her that he'd have Daddy call her.

Then, Mama took Matt's letter to Ms. Welch, but this time she went with money too.

"How did it go with Ms. Welch?", Nanny asked Mama that evening as we all gathered back home from our day.

"She took the money and said she'd look into it and do some calling around.", Mama answered as she poured herself a glass of water.

Mama opened the refrigerator and stood there in front of it, sighing as she spoke into it, "Nothing sounds good for supper.".

"What if we go out to eat tonight?", Nanny asked.

I nodded my head and smiled, "Can we, Mama?", I looked over at Mama hoping she'd say yes.

Mama looked at me and then Nanny, "Oh, I guess. We haven't been out in a while.", she smiled back at me and ran her fingers through my hair. I jumped up and down, excited to go out and eat.

"It will be nice to have someone cook for us for a change.", she added.

When we got to the diner, everyone in burgundy aprons said hello to Mama, most of them asking if she wasn't tired of the place.

Mama and I sat on one side of a booth and Nanny sat on the other side. We looked over our menus as a mother and father walked in with three young sons. Mama stared at them as they walked by and sat at the next booth beside us.

She watched them as they got settled and started looking at their menus.

A tall, skinny waitress appeared by our booth, interrupting Mama's view, "Well, hello stranger. I see you brought some special guests tonight.", she smiled at Nanny and winked at me.

Mama looked over at us and rejoined our world, "Oh, uh, yes. This is my mom and my little girl.", she told the waitress who was holding a pen and a notepad.

"Hi, mom and little girl.", she giggled as she gave us a wave with her hand, "What can I get for you tonight?".

"I think we all want burgers and fries.", Nanny told her.

I quickly spoke up, "Can I have chocolate milk? Please?", I looked at Mama.

"Oh, alright.", she smiled.

The waitress repeated our order and then winked at me as she said, "And one glass of chocolate milk.". Then she took our menus and walked off to the kitchen.

Mama gazed over at the family she had been staring at, "Wonder what they're like now?", Mama said.

Nanny looked over to see the family Mama was watching and changed the subject,"You think that man over there is handsome?", nodding towards a man who was sitting alone at the counter.

Mama looked over at him, "He's okay, I guess.", she answered.

"I'm going to try and get his attention.", Nanny stood up and smoothed out her dress, then pulled the top of it down just enough to show more cleavage. Fluffing her curls with her hands, "Wish me luck.", she said as she pranced towards the man.

Mama rolled her eyes, "Good luck.", she said.

Nanny walked over beside the man and leaned across the counter to grab some napkins, bumping into him, "Oh, excuse me, I'm sorry.", Nanny blushed, smiled and then pranced back to our booth. The man watched her over his shoulder as she came back and sat down, looking at him and giving him a shy smile. Me and Mama looked everywhere but at the man and held in our laughs.

Nanny talked about everything she could think of to keep Mama distracted from watching the family beside us. She talked about the market and how everyone stops to discuss Mama's paintings. She asked me about school and I told them about my friend wanting to have a sleepover. Everytime Mama's eyes drifted off towards the family, Nanny thought of a new topic.

Watching Mama hurt over my brothers was always hard for Nanny.

"We have to help her find her spark again, Daisy.", Nanny would say when she was worried about Mama.

Later that week, Ms. Welch finally got back to Mama.

"Uh-huh...okay...three, seven, eight, two. Got it.", Mama said on the phone as she wrote the numbers down on a piece of paper, "Thank you so much, Ms. Welch. I'll let you know.".

Nanny was on the couch reading the newspaper, "What did she say?", Nanny asked when Mama hung up the phone.

Mama came into the living room and sat next to Nanny, "She found out the name and number of the warehouse.", she said, looking at the paper she had written on.

Nanny put the newspaper down in her lap.

"There you go. Keep on fighting.", Nanny smiled.

Chapter Twenty- (Matt)

It had been a couple of years since we moved to New Mexico. Maria had taken complete control of everything in our lives. I began to hate school after I hadn't found another friend like Jake. The kids were different and I had a hard time finding my place with them. The only thing that made me feel better was to punch anyone who looked at me wrong.

I had been into several fights after school and had even been suspended once because I tripped a boy at school and then kicked him in the back. He had made fun of my hair and I lost control of myself. I knew my hair looked stupid, I didn't need him to tell me. I was home for two days, scrubbing floors and toilets with a toothbrush. By the time I was finished the tips of my fingers were beginning to bleed from cracking. "You won't get kicked out of school again, will you, boy?", Dad said while Maria stood watch, making sure I scrubbed exactly as she expected.

Maria made us keep our hair buzzed short. She'd have us sit in a chair in the kitchen one at a time while she'd shave it all off. I asked her once if I could let it grow out but she said, "Absolutely not. You'll get bugs from those kids at school. Don't you know how dirty they are?".

I didn't understand why she thought that, they all seemed clean to me, I just didn't like most of them, but then, I didn't like most anyone. The only friend I had was Carlos. He was short and chubby with black rimmed glasses and a head full of thick, jet black hair that he kept slicked back. I was jealous of his hair.

Carlos would sneak some cigarettes from his dad and we'd meet up in the alley behind the school, "Here, man", he'd say in a low, cool voice as he'd take a cigarette from his shirt pocket. I'd take it and then cup my hands around a flame while he flicked a lighter to light mine and then his cigarette. We were the coolest fifth graders in town as we puffed, squatting with our hands resting on our knees and letting the cigarettes hang from our lips out of the sides of our mouths.

Sneaking around with him was a welcomed relief from my home life. Maria expected more and more from us while she spent most of her time on the phone or the couch.

"Marcus!", she'd yell, "Bring me some water!", "Matthew! Go fold the clothes!", "Mitchell! Make the beds!", demand after demand, she went on from the time we walked into the house after school until the time we went to bed.

Marc was the only one who whined or argued every once in a while, but she reminded him who was in charge very quickly with a smack to his face or his bottom or whatever part of him she could reach.

One time, she told him that maybe he needed to know about God and put him in the hall closet with a Bible. She left him inside there for hours and told him to read something good in there. He came out with tear stained cheeks, his head sweaty. Then, he silently got to whatever chore it was she wanted him to do. She used this punishment from time to time since it seemed to work the first time. I don't think she had ever read it herself though, the Bible didn't seem to be her kind of book.

Mitch always complied, he had learned quickly to just do what she said. He had quit sucking his thumb around her after what seemed like a thousand slaps. The only time I ever saw him with it in his mouth was occasionally when he was in bed. Then there was me, who tried to do chores before she even started asking. I kept quiet and when I wasn't doing chores I stayed in my bedroom until I was called out to do something else.

The time I used to spend playing and helping my brothers turned into solitude in my bedroom, most of which was spent reading comic books or drawing, which even those things became less and less.

One day at school, my teacher gave an assignment on how to write a letter. She asked us to think about someone special to us, who did not live with us and send them an addressed letter.

Immediately, I thought of Mama. I hadn't thought of her in a while, but she hadn't quite been erased from my memory like she had been from my life.

We quit speaking of her when we moved. After never hearing from her or seeing her again, we figured Dad telling us she didn't care about us anymore must be true.

When I first attempted to write the letter I had a mission to hurt her, "Why did you leave us? I hate you and I'm glad I don't see you anymore. You are the worst mother ever.". As I poured out my anger into the letter, I felt some shame, deep down knowing that's not what I wanted to say to her. I crumpled up the paper and began writing a new letter. I wanted her to know I was thinking about her and Daisy. I wanted just to be able to tell her I still loved her whether she cared about me or not. My teacher read it when I was finished and said I did a good job. She gave me an envelope to address, but I wasn't sure what to put on it to make sure it was sent to Mama. Then, I remembered a letter I had seen that had Nanny's address on it. It was an old letter Dad had kept from before I was born that included his and Mama's birth certificates. I only had to figure out how to get a hold of it.

I devised a plan to ask Dad if he knew where Mama and her parents were born. I nervously asked him one evening at supper. He took a bite of his rigatoni and then asked, "What do you need to know that for?". Maria shot daggers at me with her eyes as she buttered a piece of bread she was holding.

"Oh, uh, I just have a report at school. And...uh...I have to know where my parents and grandparents were born.", I lied.

"It's for school?", he looked at me curiously.

"Yeah...I just need to know the places.", I answered hoping he would buy into my lie.

"I think I have something for that.", he said, "I'll go look when we're finished eating.", he added as he continued eating.

Surprised that my plan might work, I felt relieved and began quickly eating my supper with Maria's eyes on me the entire time. It felt like she knew I was up to something.

After supper, Dad came out of his room carrying the letter I needed, "Here it is.", he said, "Get what you need and give it back.".

Taking the letter, I stared at it, amazed that he believed my lie. I looked at the big manilla envelope that contained Mama's birth certificate along with Dad's.

"Thanks.", I said as I grabbed my school bag and pulled out a notebook and a pencil. Quickly, I wrote down the address that was on the front of the envelope and then pulled out the birth certificates. I wrote down the places my parents and grandparents were born and then replaced them back inside the envelope. I stuffed the notebook back into my schoolbag. I couldn't believe it worked so smoothly as I handed the envelope back to Dad. "Got what you needed?", he asked me as I nodded.

When I got to school the next day, I pulled out the notebook and the letter for Mama from my schoolbag. I carefully wrote Mama's name, Mabel Mair, and then Nanny's address on the envelope. On the top corner I wrote my name and address. Using my tongue, I sealed the letter in hopes that it might actually reach Mama or at least Nanny. I placed a stamp that my teacher had given me onto the envelope and turned it into her. She promised to mail all of our letters by the end of the week.

I was proud of myself for accomplishing such a difficult task and right under Dad's nose.

Chapter Twenty-One- (Daisy)

Mama came home from the diner and immediately went to the phone.

She opened a drawer and pulled out the paper that she had written the warehouse name and number on. As she began dialing the number, Nanny came in from working outside, "How was your day?", she asked as she came inside, slipping off her boots and setting them by the door.

Mama put her finger to her lips and waved at Nanny as she walked into the kitchen. Nanny looked over at me and then sat down at the kitchen table.

"Oh, hello, I'm wondering if you could help me. I'm looking for someone named Mike Mair who works for you.", Mama spoke into the phone, "Uh-huh, okay, yes. Tomorrow. Okay, thank you.".

She hung up the phone, "He works tomorrow. That means they're still there.", Mama told Nanny.

"So what do we do now?", Nanny asked her.

"I'm not sure. I'll ask Ms. Welch.", she answered, "But I think this means a trip to New Mexico is in order.".

Nanny smiled and waved her hands in the air, "Well, alright then! Let's get it planned."

"We're really going to New Mexico?", I asked.

"Well, not today, honey, but as soon as we can.", Mama answered.

We went on with the evening as usual with supper and then bedtime. I crawled into bed next to Mama as she turned off the lamp on the nightstand. She rolled over towards me and kissed my forehead, "Goodnight, baby girl.".

"Goodnight, Mama.", I laid there and thought about what New Mexico must be like. I imagined cowboys and Indians riding horses around creeks and through bushes like I had seen on the western shows Nanny watched on t.v., "Mama, when we get there will we see them?", I asked as I snuggled up close to her.

"Oh, honey, I hope so.", she whispered.

Mama shared her new information with Ms. Welch and she encouraged the idea of us going to New Mexico. Mama and Nanny looked at the calendar together and picked a day in the next few weeks. Nanny went around the house looking for her stashes of money. She found some in her regular hiding spots and then some in newer spots, "Oh! One more!", she pointed in the air and then opened the cabinets under the kitchen sink. There, she pulled out a basket of cleaning supplies, shuffling through them she picked up an empty box that once contained laundry detergent. She reached inside the box and pulled out a wad of cash. She carried it over to the table and began counting it along with all the other money she had found, smoothing out each bill and placing them into stacks.

Mama added the tip money she had been collecting in a jar to the table. Nanny then added it to the pile and kept counting. Mama and I stood side by side with our arms around each other, anxiously watching Nanny count.

When Nanny finished counting, she proudly announced, "Eight hundred fifty-two. I think that'll get us there, girls."

Mama and I hugged, giggling in excitement.

The next week, as we were dreaming of seeing the boys in New Mexico and planning what to pack, there was a phone call, Nanny answered, "Hello? Oh, hi Ms. Welch.", she said, "Yes, she's here. Hold on and I'll get her for you."

Nanny sat the phone down on the counter and looked at me, "Go get your mother.", she told me.

I went down the hallway and into the bedroom that Mama and I still shared to find her putting a folded shirt into a suitcase.

She looked up at me as I entered the room, "Mama, someone's on the phone for you.", I told her as she walked towards me, "Who is it?", she asked.

"I don't know. I think Ms. Welch.", I answered as she brushed past me to go answer.

I followed behind her as she went into the kitchen where Nanny was still standing beside the phone.

Mama picked up the phone, "Hello?", she said, "Oh, hi Ms. Welch. Okay.", she paused and then slumped her shoulders as she listened. She picked up the phone box and carried it, still holding the receiver to her ear and sat at the table.

"Uh-huh. Okay. Thank you.", she said as she slowly set the receiver down onto the box to hang up.

She sat there at the table, speechless.

Nanny and I joined her at the table, "What did she say, Mable?", Nanny asked.

Mama shook her head slowly and then drew her eyes towards Nanny's.

"He quit the warehouse.", Mama told her.

Nanny's jaw dropped and I sat back in my chair trying to understand what that meant.

Nanny quickly got up and grabbed her cigarettes out of her purse. As she lit one, she began pacing in circles, "That son of a...", she looked over at me, "devil.", she finished.

"Did she tell you anything else?", Nanny asked, taking a puff of her cigarette.

Mama sat there frozen, then slowly said, "She just said that she called to check up on it and the man at the warehouse told her he quit two days ago.", Mama's voice drifted, "Mike told him he was moving to Arizona.".

"Arizona.", Nanny repeated, "What's he doing?", Nanny flicked her ashes into the ashtray on the table, "He's just become a wandering fool.", she grumbled.

"He always wins.", Mama whispered and without another word she got up from the table and went to the bedroom.

As time went on, Mama began crying most of the days and speaking less. Nanny began taking me to school as Mama got up and ready for work later and later each morning. She quit eating and only smoked.

"I'm worried about her.", Nanny said to me just about everyday on the way to school.

"Maybe Bertie can help me straighten her out.", she suggested to me.

Aunt Bertie, who had moved to Alabama after the divorce, had begun a new life with a man we didn't know. Nanny didn't seem to like him and so, when Bertie left with him she became distant, rarely contacting us. When Nanny suggested her name for help, I knew she must be desperate. Nanny called Bertie and asked if she could plan a trip up to see us for a weekend.

"It'll be nice to have all of my girls together.", Nanny said to Mama when she told her about it. But, Mama only said, "Yeah, that will be nice.", which was not at all at the level of Nanny's expectation of a response.

"Oh, Mabel. Let's try to do something fun while she's here. Maybe go see a movie.", Nanny continued on about it as she tried to see some kind of life come to Mama.

One evening, while I was working on homework at the kitchen table, Nanny was cleaning up in the kitchen while Mama was in the bathroom. As I was writing the words for my spelling test we heard a loud thud. The sound was so loud it shook the walls and Nanny dropped the plate she was holding causing it to fall onto the floor and shatter. Nanny jumped over the pieces and ran to the bathroom. I sat still in my chair and listened to Nanny begin crying hysterically from the bathroom, "Oh, Mabel, what have you done!". She came running back into the kitchen and grabbed the phone, frantically dialing.

"Daisy, go get some rags out of the closet.", she told me as she began to speak on the phone loudly, "Hello? Hello? Yes, this is Peggy Culhane and I need an ambulance right away. My daughter has cut herself.". I came running back from the closet with the rags and handed them to Nanny. When I heard what she said on the phone I instantly became scared for Mama. As Nanny told her address on the phone I ran down the hall to the bathroom to check on Mama. When I got to the doorway I stopped. There was Mama on the floor, with blood around her arm and a cut on her forehead. Nanny came running back in, pushing me out of the way as she sat down on the floor next to Mama. She put the rags I had given her around Mama's wrist and held it tight as she scooted Mama into her lap. I started crying as I watched.

"Go outside and wait for the ambulance.", Nanny told me as she began rocking back and forth with Mama in her lap, patting the blood on Mama's forehead with another rag.

I ran outside and stood on the porch, believing Mama was dead. As I waited, I sat down on the porch, pulled my knees up to my chest and began rocking and crying. Waiting there felt like forever when the sound of the ambulance finally came. I could see the lights flashing in the distance through the trees as it came closer. As the ambulance pulled up to the house, I stood up and watched two men get out and go to the back, taking out a stretcher, they wheeled it up to the porch. I pointed inside the house as they rushed past me to go in, pulling the stretcher with them. Soon, a police car pulled up behind the ambulance and an officer got out. He walked up to me where I was still standing on the porch.

"Hello, little girl.", he said to me. I looked up at him, frightened by what I had just seen.

"Who's hurt in there?", he asked as he pulled out a notepad and pen from his shirt pocket.

"Mama.", I told him in a whisper.

He clicked his pen and started writing in the notepad.

"What happened to your Mama?", he asked.

"She cut herself.", I told him, "There's blood...", I began crying harder, unable to speak anymore. The officer put his arm around my shoulders and pulled me close to him, "Alright, there, it's going to be okay.", he comforted me, "They're going to get her all fixed up, okay?", he patted my back as I continued to cry.

Soon, the men with the stretcher came rolling it out the door with Mama laying on it. She had a thin, white blanket on top of her and a bandage on her forehead. One of the men was holding her bandaged wrist tightly as they wheeled the stretcher to the ambulance.

"Mama!", I cried out and started to run after the stretcher. The officer grabbed me and scooped me into his arms as I watched them put Mama into the ambulance. Nanny came up behind me and the officer, "I've got her.", she said to him as she took me from his arms and sat me down in front of her, holding me tightly.

"Thank you.", she told the officer, "I'll follow them to the hospital.".

The officer nodded, tipped his hat and patted me on the head.

Nanny grabbed my hand and began walking to the car, "Come on, now, Daisy.", she told me as she ushered me to the car.

As we followed the ambulance, I sat in the front seat with my knees curled up to my chest, watching the glow of the lights from the ambulance on the trees as we passed by them. Nanny sat straight up in her seat with her eyes set on the ambulance as she followed.

"Oh, baby girl, what are we going to do?", she spoke to the windshield, "We've got to get her back somehow.".

I was smart enough to know that once people die, you don't get them back.

When we arrived at the hospital, Nanny and I followed the ambulance drivers with Mama on the stretcher inside. As they wheeled her inside, doctors and nurses came pouring around her, talking about blood and I.V.s as they began pulling the blanket off of her quickly, getting to work.

One nurse turned to me and Nanny, directing us to a waiting area with benches, "You two wait in here and I'll come back as soon as we get her taken care of.", she told us.

Nanny and I sat down on a bench where she pulled me up into her lap, holding me tight and running her fingers through my hair just like Mama always did when she was nervous.

"Wait here a second, Daisy.", she said as she shifted out from under me on the bench. Standing up she patted my shoulder and then dug in her purse for her coin purse. She opened it up and found a dime, "I'm going to give Bertie a call real quick.".

I stayed on the bench as Nanny walked over to a row of payphones that hung on the wall.

She put the dime into the slot of one of the phones and dialed, turning around to look at me as she waited for Bertie to answer.

"Hey, baby. I know it's late.", Nanny said, "No, it's Mabel.", she looked over at me and then turned away from me, whispering something to Bertie through the phone.

"Okay, baby. Please, be careful driving.", she said just before hanging up the phone and then walked back towards me.

"Nanny?", I began as she sat back down next to me and lit a cigarette, "How did Mama cut herself?", I asked.

Nanny took a big, long puff of her cigarette, holding the smoke in her mouth for a moment before letting it blow out into a cloud above us.

"I think she must've fell on something.", she quickly thought up and then put her hand on my knee as she continued smoking.

After a while of sitting there, a doctor came into the waiting room, "Mabel Mair family.", he said, looking around at the few people who were waiting on benches. Nanny jumped up when she heard him and walked quickly over to him, "Yes, sir, right here.".

The doctor turned to Nanny and shook her hand.

"I'm her mother.", Nanny introduced herself.

He slowly smiled and nodded as he began to talk, "She lost a lot of blood before she got here. It's a good thing you found her when you did.", he told Nanny as she listened with her hands together in front of her.

"Is she going to be okay?", Nanny wrung her hands as she spoke.

"Yes, ma'am. We've got her stable and she's resting now.", he told her. Nanny took a deep breath and then let it out. She leaned over and hugged the doctor, "Oh, thank you! Thank you!", she let out as she started crying.

The doctor patted her back as she continued to hug him, "Why don't you and the girl over there go on home and get some rest too. You can come back in the morning.".

Nanny let go of him and wiped tears from her eyes.

"Ma'am, your daughter is in good hands here. She'll be fine.", he reassured.

Nanny glanced over at me and nodded, "Okay, but you promise to call if anything changes?", she asked.

"Yes, ma'am, I promise.", he told her, "Now, please, go get some sleep. She's okay now.".

The next morning, after a restless night that I'd spent sleeping with Nanny, who tossed and turned all night, we went back to the hospital to see Mama. When we went into her room, she was sitting up in the bed with a bandage wrapped around her wrist and the one on her forehead was still in place from the night before.

Mama turned to look at the door as Nanny walked in, rushing over to her side. I stepped into the room and stayed beside the door, afraid to go in any further. Nanny kissed Mama's head and then picked up her hand that was not hurt to hold. She leaned over Mama and rubbed the bandage that was wrapped around Mama's wrist.

"I'm sorry, Mom.", Mama said to Nanny, "I didn't know what else to do anymore.".

Nanny kissed Mama's head again, "Oh, honey. I understand.", she said as she patted Mama's hand she was holding, "You sure scared me though. Please, don't do that again.".

Nanny looked over at me, motioning for me to come closer, "Me and this baby girl of yours need you around.".

Mama looked over at me and began to cry, reaching her hand out to me, "Oh, Daisy, I'm so sorry. Come over here baby.".

I walked over to the side of the bed. Nanny moved out of the way as she patted the bed for me to sit next to Mama. I sat on the bed and Mama grabbed my hand.

"Did you fall, Mama?", I asked.

Mama looked into my eyes, biting her lip and then looked over at Nanny for help.

Nanny moved back over behind me and put her hand on my shoulder, "Sometimes, when you're in the middle of a battle, Daisy, you fall.", Nanny said as she looked at Mama, "But then you get back up and you keep on fighting.", she continued, "The fall isn't important, it's the getting back up that is.".

Chapter Twenty-Two- (Matt)

A month had gone by since I had sent the letter to Mama. Every once in a while I wondered if she ever got it, imagining her taking it from the mailbox and laughing in pity at me reaching out to her.

I had asked Dad once if Mama ever called us and he said no and then proceeded to remind me to move on because she doesn't care about us anymore.

I tried as hard as I could to take his advice. The best way for me to do it was to just try and hate her, but I couldn't. Instead, I just stayed angry.

I had finished my chores one evening when Carlos ended up at our front door. Maria answered the door in her pink robe.

"Is Matt home?", he asked her.

She turned and hollered at me down the hall to my bedroom where I was playing a game of solitaire. I assumed she had another chore for me to do, so I left my game and went to see.

"Yes, ma'am?", I came out of my bedroom and into the living area.

Maria looked at me and pointed outside, "You have a friend.", she said.

I looked towards the door and saw Carlos standing there through the screen door.

I looked back at Maria, "Can I?", I waited for her to answer, hoping she'd say yes.

She nodded and said, "Be back before dark.".

I ran outside as quickly as I could before she changed her mind. I hadn't had any friends over the whole time we'd been in New Mexico so I was excited to finally have one.

"Hey, man.", Carlos said to me as I hurried outside.

He was holding a soccer ball, "Want to play?", he asked as he let the ball down on the ground, kicking it to me before I could answer.

Soccer was something I'd never played in Michigan and I hadn't been interested in playing since being in New Mexico.

After several failed attempts at catching the ball with my feet when Carlos would pass it to me, I kicked it as hard as I could down the street, "This is stupid!", I shouted.

"That's my ball, man!", he yelled as he chased it down the street.

Feeling bad about kicking the ball so hard, I ran behind Carlos to help him go get it. It rolled up into a yard across the street where he captured it and turned around, "Why'd you do that?", he asked as he ran back to me.

I shrugged my shoulders, "I didn't mean to.", I lied.

"Oh, well, you want to walk down to the store and get some candy?", he then asked.

"I don't have any money.", I told him.

"I don't either, man.", he gave a sneaky smile and started down the street, "Come on!", he waved for me to follow him. We walked a few streets down until we made it to a corner store and went inside.

"Follow me.", he whispered as he walked down the aisle with candy. I followed him as he stood in front of rows of candy, picking up one candy bar and then another, putting them down as if to be deciding what he wanted. Then, he looked both ways down the aisle and grabbed a Baby Ruth and put it in his pocket.

"Well, go on, man.", he nudged me.

I looked up and down the aisle and then grabbed the first candy bar I saw and slipped it into my pocket just as Carlos had done.

"Okay, come on.", he said as he turned to walk back out of the store. I followed him out, looking behind me, waiting to get caught.

When we got outside of the store we both started running back towards my house. Once we got to my street, we stopped to catch our breath and then looked at each other. We started laughing, as we proudly pulled the stolen candy out of our pockets and began unwrapping them. The taste of not getting caught was so sweet. As we got back to my house, I put the last piece in my mouth, "I better go in now.", I said with my mouth full.

"Okay, man. See you at school.", he said as he turned to walk back home. I went inside and walked straight back to my room. As I passed by Maria who was sitting on the couch, I felt guilty and thought she must have known what I did when she asked, "Where did you two go?".

I stuttered with my answer, "Umm...oh...we...uh...we just walked around...and...uh... played soccer.".

"Hmm.", was all she said as she went back to watching t.v.

I went into my bedroom to find Marc and Mitch playing with the cards I had left out on the floor.

"What are you playing?", I asked them.

"War.", Marc answered as he flipped a card over.

"Can I play next?", I asked.

They both nodded as they continued playing. I thought about my achievement as I waited my turn, relaxing on the bed.

A few days later, Dad came home from working at the warehouse. He walked into the house and went straight past the kitchen filled with the aroma of tomato sauce. He went to his bedroom to change out of his work clothes. When he came back into the living area where us boys were watching t.v. and waiting for supper, "Boys.", he said, "When we finish supper I need you to go pack up your rooms.". We looked around at each other as he walked outside and then came back in carrying boxes. He set the boxes on the floor in front of us.

"Why, Daddy?", Mitch asked.

"Yeah, why? Are we moving?", Marc joined in. Dad walked into the kitchen without answering them and put his arms around Maria who was busy stirring sauce on the stove.

"You ready?", he asked her as she continued stirring.

She nodded her head and reached to turn off the stove.

"Maybe she'll finally leave us alone when we get there.", Maria commented as she began preparing our plates, mumbling some Italian words under her breath.

Marc and Mitch went to the table to sit and I followed, disappointed about the news of another move. I had finally made a friend and now we were moving again.

As we all sat and began to eat Mitch asked, "Where are we going, Daddy?".

Dad looked up from his plate, "Arizona.".

Arizona?, I thought.

Marc followed Mitch's question with, "When?".

"We leave tomorrow night.", Dad answered.

I began poking at the pasta on my plate, no longer hungry. Maria slapped the table in front of me as soon as she noticed, "Eat.", she said with her eyes squinted.

"Why are we going to Arizona? What about school tomorrow?", Marc continued to question.

Dad looked over at Marc, "Nunya.", he answered with a smirk and took another bite of the pasta on his plate. Maria let out a giggle at Dad's answer.

When supper was over and I had finished the dishes, I headed to my bedroom with a box. Looking around, I began with my comic books, tossing them into the box. I took the lamp off of my dresser and just as I was about to add it to the box, I started to feel angry.

I had just gotten used to this school and had worked so hard to earn respect with my punches, even finally having a friend come over and now we were moving?

I took the lamp and threw it towards the wall where it busted and slid down to the floor.

Feeling some sort of relief, I looked around for something else to throw. I picked up some toy cars off of the floor and threw them one at a time at the wall. As they each bounced off of the wall and landed back on the floor, realizing they wouldn't break, I gave up. I sat on my bed and punched the mattress, harder and harder with every hit.

Marc appeared at my door, peaking in.

"What do you want?", I scolded. He walked away as I got up to slam the door behind him.

I turned around to go back to my bed when something in the closet caught my eye. It was the blue bag from Mama. I went over to the closet and reached up for the bag that was laying high on a shelf. I grabbed it into my arms and squeezed, hugging it as tightly as I could, imagining it was Mama. I closed my eyes and tried to remember the details of her face. Her deep brown eyes, her soft skin, the dimples in her cheeks with tiny freckles on her nose. I refused to cry as I stood there with tears welling up in my eyes, so I stopped hugging the bag and tossed it into the box as the vision of Mama disappeared from my mind.

The next evening, after everything was packed up in the house, Dad rubbed his hands together, "Okay. I think we're ready to start filling the trailer.", he told me and my brothers, "Start with these.", he directed as he began handing us boxes.

Knowing a long night of driving was ahead of us, I reluctantly began carrying boxes to the trailer.

Maria helped Dad carry our furniture and heavy things out to load.

When we finished loading everything, once again, the back of the car piled with things up to the roof. It was dark as we got into the car and drove away with the Adobe house behind us, growing smaller in the rearview mirror.

Chapter Twenty-Three- (Daisy)

When Mama came home from the hospital with Nanny, Bertie was waiting with me inside the house.

Together, we made a strawberry cake with chocolate frosting, Mama's favorite, to welcome her back.

As soon as she walked in the door, I ran up to her with a bouquet of wildflowers that Nanny and I had picked earlier in the day. I jumped up into her arms in excitement to see her, nearly knocking her down as she hugged me and giggled.

"Here, Mama, these are for you.", I said as I handed her the flowers. She set down her purse and took them from me, putting them to her nose to smell.

"Oh, aren't these so beautiful?", she smiled as she spoke, "Now, how did you know I love daisies?", she winked.

I put my hands to my mouth and grinned.

"Oh, we also have something for you in the kitchen.", I told her.

Mama looked at me surprised, "Really?".

I grabbed her hand to lead her into the kitchen, "Uh-huh, close your eyes until I say.", I couldn't wait to show her the cake. I had worked so hard to make sure it was perfect.

Mama closed her eyes as I led her to the table, "Are they still closed?", I bossed.

"Yes!", she laughed.

"Okay, here's the chair.", I put her hand on the back of the chair so she could feel it to sit down.

"Can I open them?", she asked as she giggled.

"No! Not yet!", I commanded.

Nanny and Bertie followed us into the kitchen as Mama slowly felt her way into the chair to sit.

Once she was sitting at the table in front of the cake, "Okay, now!", I told her.

She opened her eyes to see the pink frosted cake on the table with a card next to it.

Putting her hand to her chest, smiling, "Oh, wow, you shouldn't have.", she turned the plate that the cake was sitting on to admire it, "You did this for me?".

" Uh-huh, and this.", I reached over to pick up the card.

Mama looked around at Nanny, Bertie and I, smiling as she opened the card. I had drawn a picture inside of me and her with some hearts around us. Nanny wrote a message, 'Get up and keep fighting baby. We love you.', it said.

Bertie signed it too, 'Sisters no matter what and friends forever.', she wrote.

After reading the card, Mama closed it and ran her fingers over the front, "Thank you all. Really, it means so much.", she stood up and hugged each of us and then we all gathered together for one big group hug with all three women in tears.

They began laughing at each other and teasing one another about all of them crying.

"Okay, okay, now that we've settled all that, let's have cake.", Nanny said with a giggle.

Nanny cut each of us a piece as Bertie poured us all a glass of milk.

We sat at the table eating and talking about how delicious it was.

It was so good to have Mama back after a few days without her and I was so thankful she was still alive.

Later in the week, near the end of Bertie's visit, she began talking to Mama about Alabama during a game of checkers.

"You should come down this summer.", she suggested, "Get away for a little while.".

"Oh, I don't know.", Mama replied, "What about Mom?".

Bertie waved her hand, "Oh, come on, Mabel, I think she can handle herself.". She grabbed Mama's arm, "Come on, just go down there for a little while. It'll be good for you.", Bertie begged.

Mama shook her head at Bertie, "Let me think about it.". Taking one of her pieces on the checkerboard, Mama used it to jump over one of Bertie's pieces and then another and another, "Now, king me.", Mama smirked at Bertie.

Eventually, Bertie went back to Alabama and Mama's wrist healed within a few weeks. She had started back to work and everything started falling back into place. Summer was coming soon and I was looking forward to being out of school so I could start going back to the market with Nanny. I missed watching the people walking through and all the sights and sounds of the things being sold. One morning, Nanny was driving me to school when she asked, "Daisy, what do you think about going to Alabama this summer?".

I wrinkled my nose at the thought of it, "I don't know.".

She nudged my elbow, "You could play with your cousins there. Wouldn't you like that?", she glanced over at me for a reply.

"But what about you?", I asked.

Nanny pulled up to the front of the school and parked, "Oh, Daisy, I'm a big girl. You don't have to worry about me, baby girl.", she looked over and smiled at me.

"But, I'll miss you.", I looked back at her sadly.

She reached over and rubbed my head, "Well, I'll miss you too, but sometimes, when you're fighting a battle, you have to change positions so you can see better.", she patted my knee, "I think that's what your Mama needs.".

I looked down at her hand on my knee and mumbled, "Yeah, maybe.".

She patted my knee, "Just think about it while you're in there getting smarter.", she smiled.

I nodded my head as she looked in the rearview mirror to fluff out her curls, "Now, get on in there, before you're late.", she told me as she spoke into the mirror, looking at her reflection.

I couldn't imagine being away from her and I didn't want to.

As the days turned into weeks, Mama came home from the diner one evening and sat down at the kitchen table while Nanny started supper.

"You won't believe who came in to see me today.", Mama said.

Nanny was throwing some flour covered chicken into a skillet. As it crackled and popped she turned to look at Mama, "Oh? Who?", she asked.

"Becky.", she answered.

Nanny looked confused, "Becky? You mean little Becky?".

Mama nodded her head, "Yes, well, she's not so little anymore. That pretty little thing has turned into a beautiful little woman.", she said.

Nanny turned back to the skillet to tend to the chicken, "Oh my, I bet so. Did you talk to her?".

Mama folded her hands on the table, "Yeah, we talked about how she's met some boy and getting married.", Mama told her, "We talked about Joe and Bess. He's still doing good with his business.".

Nanny pulled the chicken out of the skillet and set it all in a neat pile on a plate. As she carried the plate of chicken to the table, it was still crackling. Mama began to reach for a piece when Nanny swatted her hand away, "Not yet, let it cool a little.". Mama pulled her hand back, "Oh, alright.", she huffed.

Nanny wiped her hands on the apron she was wearing and sat down at the table, "Well, go on. What else did she have to say?".

Mama leaned over the table, "She said they were in Arizona for a little while but the job he got there wasn't working out so they went back to New Mexico.".

Nanny listened intently while she fanned the chicken with her hand.

"She also told me that she didn't like the woman he's with and apparently they got married while they were in New Mexico the first time.", Mama went on, "Her name's Maria and she's some Italian woman he met a long time ago.".

"Mistress Maria from Italy.", Nanny mocked as she rolled her eyes.

"He was seeing her all that time.", Mama added, "Accusing me of cheating, when it was him all along.".

Nanny sat back in her chair and lit a cigarette, "Well, of course, that's what cheaters do. They have to take the attention off what they're doing somehow.".

Mama took a cigarette from Nanny and lit it, "Anyway, she said that Maria's a witch and has Mike under a spell.".

Nanny took a puff of her cigarette and exhaled, "Well, I don't think anyone could put that man under a spell. Sounds to me he's just found an equal partner.".

"Yeah.", Mama replied.

Nanny put her cigarette out in the ashtray, "I think we can quit babysitting this chicken and eat it.". She got up from the table to get a bowl filled with salad and some plates.

"Come on in here, Daisy!", Mama called to me.

As we ate our supper, Mama decided to talk some more about going to Alabama,

"Daisy, I've got us a few weeks planned. As soon as school's out, we'll go spend some time with Bertie.".

I set down the chicken leg I was eating and looked at Mama, "Okay, but will we come back in time for me to go with Nanny to the market?".

Mama giggled, "You love that market just as much as Nanny, don't you?".

Nanny joined Mama's giggle, "I'm not sure which one she'll miss more, little old me or the market.".

Chapter Twenty-Four- (Matt)

We stayed in Arizona for a little less than a year when we moved back to a different town in New Mexico. It was so hot in Arizona I was glad to get out of there, at least it was a little cooler in New Mexico. It was there, in Arizona, that I began junior high and in the middle of my second semester, we up and moved again after Dad got laid off from the warehouse he had been working at there. He got into an argument with some guy and punched him.

I would be starting high school next year and had begun to dream about life after I could get out of the house. I dreamed of being eighteen and on my own.

Marc and Mitch became closer as time went by, me, not so much. I stayed to myself while the two of them were stuck together like glue.

I had just become a teenager and they were still doing little kid stuff even though they weren't much younger than me. In Arizona, I had made a couple of friends who showed me how to ditch class to smoke in the boys' bathroom. They taught me how to climb up on the sink and shimmy open the small window that was at the top of the wall. The three of us spent a lot of time in there, picking on random boys who came in to use it.

"Stall's taken.", my friend, Paul, stood in front of the stall when a short, little red headed boy came in to use the urinal. Paul was tall and skinny with long, brown, curly hair always wearing a bandana around his forehead. I was jealous of his curls since Maria was still shaving my head. My other friend, Ron, had a shaggy wave of blonde hair and freckles.

The unsuspecting boy went to the next urinal where Ron stood in front of it also with his arms crossed. As the boy turned to go to the next urinal, I pushed in front of him, "Nope", I laughed.

Suddenly, Paul grabbed the backpack off of the boy's shoulder, "What ya got in here?", he began unzipping the backpack.

"Just some books.", the boys said.

"Lame.", said Paul as he tossed the backpack over the boy's head to Ron. Ron then threw it to me as the boy tried reaching for it. We heard the door open and I quickly threw the backpack as hard as I could at the boy, knocking him down. A teacher came in as the boy got up off the floor and scurried out. The teacher watched as the boy scurried by and then looked at the three of us, "Everything okay in here?", he asked.

Paul cleared his throat, "Oh, uh, yes, sir.", and the three of us walked out of the bathroom. We laughed all the way down the hall and then went separate ways back to our classes.

After school, I went home to find Marc and Mitch getting whooped with a belt. Maria had them both over the couch and was hitting as hard as she could, over and over, with each whip shouting, "Don't...you...ever...do...that...again!". They were both crying and were squirming with each hit.

She stopped when I walked in, pushing her hair out of her face, "Now go to your room!", she pointed to their room as they ran off holding their backs and bottoms. Then, Maria said some words in Italian and looked over at me, "Where have you been?", she scolded.

"I had to stay after.", I lied. I had really been at Ron's house listening to music.

She shook her head and headed into the kitchen to start making supper.

I went to my brothers' room to see what the whooping was about. Standing in the doorway I saw them each huddled in their beds crying.

"What did you guys do?", I asked.

"Go away!", Mitch yelled as he continued crying.

I shrugged my shoulders and went on to my bedroom.

I laid down in my bed and took a lighter out of my pocket. As I listened to them crying through the wall, I began flicking the lighter. With each flick I watched the flame rise from the lighter and then go back down as I let go.

I began thinking about leaving, imagining myself packing a bag and running away, hitchhiking to get anywhere else. Suddenly, I remembered the blue bag I had been carrying around with each move since we left Michigan. I got up out of the bed and began pulling things out of my closet to search for it. Tossing blankets and sweaters into the floor, I found some old comic books where underneath was the blue bag. I pulled it out and stared at it. It was a little worn out on the bottom with black scuff marks. The brightness of its blue color had faded. I held it open and thought about Mama. Remembering her giving me the bag, I closed my eyes tight, trying to see her face. Her brown eyes and dark hair were all I could see in my mind. I wondered where she was and if she ever thought about me. Quickly, anger started rising as I thought about how she had left us, abandoned, as Dad always said. As her shy smile appeared in my mind, I pulled the bag until it ripped.

"Forget about her.", I ripped the bag again, "She doesn't love you.", repeating everything I'd heard Dad say. I continued ripping the bag until it was in pieces. Holding them in my hands I realized that bag was the only piece of her I still had. I took out the lighter I had put back into my pocket, it was time to move on from her. Filled with anger, I held the lighter to a strand of the bag and lit the flame. As the flame singed the ends of the strand, I continued burning it until a flame caught onto it. I threw the pieces of the bag on the floor and watched as the flame took over and began to grow. Realizing what I had done, I started stomping on the flames to put them out. I quickly reached down and grabbed a small piece of the bag that had not burned yet and shoved it into my pocket. I kept stomping on the flames but they began to spread and quickly took over, consuming the sweaters and blankets I had thrown on the floor. Panicking, I ran out of my bedroom and into the kitchen to grab a pitcher of water. Maria was standing at the stove as I ran in and flung open the cabinet doors beside her. Searching for a pitcher, she turned, "Boy, what are you doing?", she snapped, "Get out of here."

Without responding to her, I found a pitcher and started filling it with water from the sink.

Just then, Marc and Mitch came running in yelling, "Fire! There's a fire!". Maria stopped what she was doing, dropping the spoon she had been using into the pot of sauce on the stove. She ran to the bedrooms and quickly came back with smoke billowing out behind her, "Out!", she pointed to the front door. We all ran out of the house as smoke poured out behind us. When we got outside, Marc, Mitch and I stood beside a tree in the front yard while Maria ran to the house next door. The three of us stood there watching as smoke rose into the sky above our house.

"What happened?", Mitch asked.

I said nothing as I stood there wondering what kind of trouble I was going to be in.

We heard sirens in the distance as Dad pulled up, just getting home from work. He jumped out of the car and ran over to where we were standing, "Where's Maria?", he asked us. We pointed towards the neighbors' house.

"What happened?", he paced in circles as he watched the smoke thicken and flames began coming out of the windows.

Soon, Maria came out with the neighbors and ran over beside us as a fire truck drove up our street and stopped in front of our house. The squeal of the sirens caused more neighbors to come out of their houses. They stood in their yards and watched as the firemen jumped out of their truck and hooked a big hose to a fire hydrant. They quickly got to work spraying water onto the house.

"What happened?", Dad asked again.

I stood silent as Maria answered, "I don't know. I was cooking and then...", her voice trailed off as she looked at me, "What did you do?", she glared at me.

I remained silent, wondering if I would go to jail for this.

When the firemen finally got the fire out, one of them came over to where we were standing.

"So, it will be a little while as we check around in there.", he said to Dad, "Do you know what caused this?".

"I have no idea. I just got home from work.", Dad answered.

The fireman looked over at Maria waiting for her to answer.

"I don't know. I was cooking.", she told him.

Then, the firemen looked at the three of us boys, "What about you? Were you in the house when this happened?", he asked us.

Marc nodded, "Yes, sir.".

Mitch spoke up, "We were in our room.".

I remained silent as everyone gave their answers.

"I'm glad you all made it out.", the fireman said to us as he walked back towards the house. Maria continued glaring at me with her arms crossed. I looked down at my feet as worry set in about what kind of punishment I would receive.

Eventually, the firemen had an idea of what happened when they found my lighter next to a pile of ashes in my bedroom. As they pulled Dad and Maria to the side to talk to them, they both looked in my direction. I kept my head down, not knowing what was next to come. To my surprise they didn't arrest me but they did have a talk with all three of us boys about the decision to play with a lighter. Marc and Mitch listened and responded with, "Yes, sir.", even though they had no idea what I'd done.

We stayed in a hotel for the next few weeks, miserably.

Marc and Mitch shared a bed next to Dad and Maria while I slept on the floor.

"No blanket for you down there.", Maria told me.

She and Dad had acted like I didn't exist while we stayed in the hotel. They walked past me without speaking and when everyone sat around to eat sandwiches, I was only given a piece of bread. With their backs turned to me as they ate, Marc and Mitch looked over their shoulders at me every once in a while. Maria only glared at me.

After a box of clothes had been donated to us, Marc and Mitch were able to wear them to school. I was only allowed to wear the clothes I was still wearing when I started the fire. I would have much rathered having the belt than the punishment they were giving me.

At school, we had an assembly with all the grade levels of the junior high packed into the auditorium. They discussed the fire, telling everyone what we had all already seen on the news and in the newspaper.

"Kids playing with a lighter.", was the start of the discussion as everyone in the auditorium glanced around to look at me and my brothers, snickering. I looked down at my lap as I sat there, enduring it all, in my filthy clothes which still had a faint scent of smoke.

I wished I would have packed the bag and left instead, so I could be miles from where I was.

Dad finally found a house for us and this time there were only two bedrooms so I shared it with my brothers. It didn't matter to me too much until summer came and we were out of school. I wasn't allowed to go to Ron's house anymore since we got caught smoking in his bedroom. So, I spent most of the summer at home. Maria had me mow lawns in the neighborhood. When I brought home the money I made, she'd put out her hand, waiting for me to give it to her, "You'll be paying for that fire for a long time.", she'd say.

Marc and Mitch started spending more time inside watching t.v. when they weren't doing chores. We were allowed one show a day and we usually all agreed on Batman.

One day, Maria had gotten in the shower while we watched our show. I had noticed her purse sitting on the floor with some money poking out of the top. I went over to where it was sitting and looked around to make sure Marc and Mitch weren't watching. As I walked past it, I bumped into the table next to it, knocking off some magazines. I bent down to pick them up and quickly pulled the money out of the purse. I shoved the money in my pocket and straightened the magazines back onto the table.

Then, I went to the bedroom and took the money out to count it. Forty dollars. I smiled, thinking of all the things I could buy.

The next day, while Maria was running errands, I asked Marc and Mitch if they wanted to go to the store.

"But we're not supposed to leave.", Mitch said.

"Who's going to know?", I asked him.

Marc shrugged his shoulders, "He's right, Mitch.".

We both stood there looking at Mitch who was unsure about going.

"No one will know if we hurry.", I told him. I walked to the front door, "Are you coming or not?", I looked back to ask Mitch.

He stayed where he was as I walked to the front door, "Suit yourself.", I shrugged and Marc followed behind me as we left the house to begin walking to the store. When we got a few houses down the street, Mitch came running up behind us, "Wait up!", he hollered as he caught up to us.

I smiled as he joined us, rubbing his head, "Oh, the little girl decided to come after all.", I laughed.

"Shut up!", Mitch said back.

We walked until we got to a gas station. I pulled the money out of my pocket and held it out for my brothers to see, "Get whatever you want.".

With their eyes wide, Marc smiled, "Where'd you get that?".

Mitch's smile turned into a look of concern, repeating Marc, "Yeah...where'd you get that?".

I smiled as I waved the money in their faces, "Nunya.", I said, "Do you want something or not?".

I turned and walked into the gas station as they followed. Marc pushed past me through the door, running as if we were in a race towards a shelf full of candy. Mitch walked behind me slowly with his hands in his pockets.

A man at the register watched us come in, leaning over the counter he told Marc to stop running. I stopped in front of the candy and began looking it over, deciding what I wanted, slow and cool. I felt like an adult for a moment, like I could do whatever I pleased, I was beginning to look like one too, so that helped. I grabbed a few candy bars and then a bag of chips as Marc reached for everything in sight, piling candy and chips in his arms. Mitch stood behind me nervously looking around.

As I walked over to the rows of large glass doors filled with drinks I looked at Mitch and nodded, "Well, go on. Get something.", I told him. I opened one of the glass doors and reached for a soda. As I walked back towards Mitch, Marc ran past me to get a drink with his arms still full of candy and chips, dropping a few on the floor. Mitch carried two candy bars in his hand as he walked over to get a drink also.

Clearing my throat to make sure my voice didn't crack, I spoke in my deepest, manly-est voice, "Alright, let's get going.".

I walked up to the register and laid everything I had chosen onto the counter. Marc followed, dumping everything in his arms out onto the counter as it spilled over the things I had just set down. Mitch walked up and gently placed the two candy bars and soda he had chosen next to the pile.

The man behind the counter looked suspiciously at us, "Will that be all?".

I reached for a pack of gum that was sitting by the register and tossed it in the pile, "Yep.", I said, pulling the money from my pocket.

The man kept eyeballing us as he rang up each item on the counter.

We walked out, carrying bags full of our treasure. We each drank our sodas and ate some of our candy as we walked back home.

"Not a word.", was all I said to them as we went back inside our house. They followed me inside and straight to our bedroom where I stashed the bags inside the corner of the closet, covering them with a blanket.

Later that day, Maria came back, slamming the front door behind her. She began walking around the house searching for something. Mitch and I were sitting on the couch as we watched her walk from room to room, moving things around in her search.

As she picked up the magazines from the table to look underneath them, Marc came out of the bedroom holding a bag of chips. He popped a chip into his mouth as Maria looked up at him. She glared at him and stomped over to him. "Where did you get this?", she snatched the bag out of his hand.

Marc slowly finished chewing the chip and glanced over at me, shrugging his shoulders. Maria slapped his cheek as he chewed, "Answer me, boy!".

Marc rubbed his cheek and again shrugged his shoulders.

She grabbed him by the ear, twisting it as he fell to his knees in pain. He began crying, "I don't know!", he whaled.

"You liar!", she yelled at him as she began hitting the top of his head.

As he cried, he attempted to block every hit with his hands on his head. Me and Mitch watched in silence from the couch. Finally, I stood up and said, "It was me.".

Maria stopped with her hand in the air, turning to look at me.

"It was me. I gave it to him.", I bravely spoke up with my chest poked out, ready to take whatever came next like a man.

"Where did you get this?", she walked closer to me and shoved the bag of chips in my face.

"I found some money and bought it.", I half lied.

"And where did you find money for it?", she asked with her hand on her hip.

"I...I...found it in your purse.", I looked her straight in the eyes.

She said nothing as she grabbed my hand and walked me almost at a jog to the kitchen.

"You mean you stole it from my purse.", she said through her teeth as she turned on the stove. The flame rose on one of the burners as she pulled my hand towards it.

"You sure do like playing with fire don't you, boy?", she glared. Quickly, she pulled my hand over the flame. I tried to pull my hand away but she pulled harder, pushing my hand onto the flame. As it burned my skin, I let out a scream and a curse word. She let go of my hand and smacked the side of my head. I grabbed my hand and started blowing on it to cool it off. Looking at my hand, the skin was beginning to bubble and some places were bright red with blood. I went to the sink, turned on the water and stuck my hand under the faucet. I held back tears as my pain turned into anger.

"That's what happens when you steal.", she said as she turned off the burner and walked away.

Chapter Twenty-Five- (Daisy)

The few weeks Mama had planned for us to be in Alabama turned into a few more weeks and then a few more until it turned into years. Once we got there, Mama decided she loved it so much she didn't want to leave.

She found us a little house, close enough for me to walk to school, where the two of us managed to somehow survive without Nanny. I missed Nanny terribly and at first, cried almost everyday for her. She called me every week and sent me letters in the mail. I'd tell her about school and she'd give me updates on the market.

Mama got a job working at a supermarket nearby and by the time I was in junior high, her and Bertie had a ritual of going to the Bingo hall once a week.

She started wearing bell bottoms, which were the first pants I'd ever seen her wear out in public. Her hair had a little gray coming in and she still never left the house without lipstick.

Her search for the boys had come out empty handed time and time again. The last we had heard, they were back in New Mexico.

She had even called the newspaper when she found out what city they were living in and asked if she could put in an advertisement for them.

"I talked to Becky yesterday.", Mama had told Nanny on the phone, "They moved back to New Mexico.".

She sat on the couch one evening as she talked, filing her fingernails.

"Yes, the longest place so far.", she went on, "I called the newspaper down there and they said I could put an advertisement in the classifieds.". She paused and glanced over at me, sitting on the other end of the couch as I worked on homework, then continued talking on the phone.

"I know...I got the idea from Bertie. Oh, I just asked them if I could put in something that said I'm looking for three teenage boys, Matthew, Marcus and Mitchell Mair. Oh, and my phone number."

When she finished talking to Nanny I asked, "Do you think it will work?".

She looked over at me and said, "Oh, Daisy, I hope so."

Then, I asked, "It's been so long though. How do we even know what they look like now?".

Mama went back to filing her fingernails, "Well, I suppose they look a whole lot like their beautiful sister.", she smiled at me.

Shrugging my shoulders, "Maybe. But, Mama, why...", I paused thinking about how to ask about Daddy.

Noticing my hesitation, "Go on, ask me anything. You're old enough to know all the answers now.", she put down the nail file and turned to give me her full attention.

I closed the school book I was holding and set it down beside me, "Okay...", I took a deep breath, "Is he really my father?", I asked with caution.

"Oh, baby girl, of course he's your father. Who else could it be?", she answered.

I looked into her eyes, "Well...then...why did he never want me?".

Mama looked down at her hands as if the answer to my question was written on them, "I have no idea except for that he didn't think he could have girls.", she looked up at me and reached over to put her hand under my chin, "But he is the one missing out on something special and I'm so glad I have you. Don't you ever think twice about that."

"Do you think we'll ever see them again?", I then asked.

Putting her hand back in her lap, she answered, "I hope so. All I've ever dreamed of is to see them again. Who knows, maybe they'll see my ad in the paper and call."

"Yeah, maybe so.", I agreed with uncertainty.

A few months went by and Mama had started learning how to play the guitar. She'd sit and pluck at it every chance she got.

"Daisy, you can always learn something new. You just have to try. ", she told me.

She loved trying everything she could and always seemed to pick up every new thing with ease. Even her paintings had gotten more detailed over time and people began wanting them as gifts.

Mama was, as Bertie always said, "Something else.". As I grew into my teenage years she became my best friend. We didn't always see eye to eye, but whether I liked to admit it at the time or not, she was the one person who I enjoyed the most. We spent time putting makeup on each other as I was learning how to use it. Together, we went shopping at the mall, trying on all the shoes and walking around in front of each other in dresses from the racks, "What about this one?", we'd ask each other as we came out of the fitting room.

When we got the call one evening from Bertie saying Nanny was in the hospital and not doing too good, Mama was the one I clung to. The three of us drove to Michigan to see Nanny as she was fading away from our lives.

When we got to the hospital, Nanny was asleep. We stood around her, taking turns holding her hand and whispering in her ear how much we loved her. I never imagined ever seeing Nanny so frail. As she began to drift further from us until there was no more breath in her, we stood there, embracing each other in tears.

Losing Nanny was my first real heartbreak and Mama's second after losing the boys. As the days went on, we took turns holding each other and drying each other's eyes.

Mama kept a necklace of Nanny's around her neck, rubbing the ruby red stone that hung from it, she whispered her thoughts as though she was talking straight to Nanny.

Eventually, Mama was constantly holding a cigarette, never seen without one between her fingers, especially when she was teaching me how to drive. Her body would jerk with every stop and go while she sat next to me.

She'd cough as she laughed and sometimes hollered, "Slow, slow, slow!", as she put her foot on the dash.

One time, she started coughing so much, blood came spitting out of her mouth.

I pulled the car over to stop, "Mama?", I said, looking at the blood on her hand.

"Oh, it's nothing. I'm fine.", she said, "Now, go on, drive us home. Don't worry about me.", she told me.

But, as I drove us back home, I did. I worried about her. The worry of that day turned into worry every day.

The more she coughed out blood, the more I worried.

"Mama, would you please just go see a doctor about that.", I insisted.

Even Bertie was getting concerned about it, "Mabel, that's not normal.", she told her as Mama spit blood into a tissue one day in front of her. They were heading to the Bingo hall when Mama had just finished fluffing out her hair and straightening her blouse.

Looking into a pocket mirror she had pulled from her purse, Mama dabbed lipstick onto her lips, "Oh, Bertie, I'm fine. You sound just like Daisy.", she said frustrated.

"Now, are we going or not?", she asked as she lit a cigarette and walked to the door.

Mama was rushed to the hospital by an ambulance the next day when she kept coughing up blood and then passed out where I found her lying on the floor by the toilet. Instantly, I was taken back to the time when I was a little girl seeing blood around her arm, thinking she was dead.

I rode with her in the ambulance and followed the drivers into the hospital who rolled her inside on a stretcher.

A nurse stopped me and directed me to a waiting room. So much of this was familiar, like I was stuck in some weird dream, as I sat down alone. The only difference this time was that there was no Nanny there to comfort me.

I called Bertie on a payphone just as Nanny had done before and then waited.

When Bertie got there, worried, she asked, "What's going on?".

I shrugged my shoulders, "They haven't told me anything yet.".

Bertie walked over to the counter in the front of the waiting room, "Excuse me.", she said to a nurse who was walking past, stopping when she heard Bertie.

"Do you have any information on my sister? Her name is Mabel. Mabel Mair.", Bertie asked.

The nurse picked up a clipboard from the counter and flipped through some papers, "Umm...yes...Mabel Mair. The doctor should be out soon to let you know something.", was all she said.

Bertie huffed and walked back to where I was sitting. She paced around the waiting room until finally a doctor came out, "Are you Bertie?", he asked her.

Bertie turned towards him, "Yes, sir.", she nodded as I stood to join her.

The doctor looked at me, "You must be Mabel's daughter.", he said.

I nodded my head and waited for him to tell us about Mama.

He pointed back to where I had just been sitting, "Why don't we have a seat?".

Bertie and I sat down in the chairs as he sat across from us and slowly began talking, "Okay, so I need to tell you both something very important.".

"Is my Mama dead?", I interrupted.

He put a hand up, "Oh, no, no, no.", he waved his hand, "Your mother is fine for right now, sweetheart.".

Relieved, I sat back in my chair waiting for what he had to say next.

"The reason your mother was coughing up blood, well, after looking at her x-rays, she has cancer in her lungs.", he told us.

Bertie stood up, "I knew it. Oh, my God, I knew those cigarettes were going to kill her.", she said as she put her hand on her forehead.

I looked at the doctor, "She has cancer? So, that means she's going to die?", I asked confusedly, waiting for him to tell me that he said that wrong or that he had gotten Mama mixed up with another patient.

Instead, he nodded his head, "I'm sorry.".

Bertie sat back down next to me, "Can we see her?", she asked.

The doctor stood up, "Yes, of course. Give us a few minutes to get her situated and I'll have a nurse come get you when she's ready.".

He began walking away then turned to look back at us, "Again, I'm really sorry.".

Bertie and I didn't speak as we waited for the nurse. I thought about what I was going to do without Mama when I was still trying to figure out what to do without Nanny. When we were called by a nurse to follow, Bertie and I walked down a long hall behind her. Mama was sitting in a bed as we walked in, "Well I guess I've done it again.", she said as we walked in.

"Yes, you have.", Bertie said to her.

"Did they tell you?", Mama asked us.

Bertie nodded her head as I stood in the corner of the room with my arms crossed, wanting to believe this was all a part of the dream I felt stuck in.

Mama came home with what seemed like hundreds of medications and a definite limit on her life. Six months.

In that time, she pressed harder to find the boys, even on days when she was feeling her worst. I'd come home from high school to find her surrounded by papers with notes and numbers she had written.

"Any luck?", I'd ask her.

Most days the answer was a disappointing, "No.", but sometimes she had a little more information.

"They're somewhere in New York.", she said.

Surprised, I asked, "New York? What could they be doing there?".

"I can't imagine...", Mama said, "But, both Joe and Becky have said that's where they are. Becky said Matt joined the Army and Marc is in the Air Force.".

"So, do they know how to find them?", I asked.

"Well, that's the problem. Joe said he's tried finding out how to get a hold of them, but Mike's wife keeps stalling on giving him any information.".

"And Becky?", I asked.

Mama shrugged, "She said the same. She said that that woman made life hard for the boys. She told me she tried to get them a few times for the summer but that woman kept them busy. All Becky really had to say about the woman was that she was no good.".

I listened to Mama, trying to think of why this woman wouldn't help.

At this point, I had barely any recollection of them. Mama still had the picture of the three of them sitting beside her bed and still talked to them as if they were there. It was so old now, it was starting to yellow. The chubby, baby faces that stared back at me when I looked at it were all I thought of when we talked about them. I had a hard time imagining what they could look like now, all grown up. Mitch should be finishing high school while Marc and Matt are grown men out there, somewhere in the world, entering their twenties.

Mama was so close to finding them as she got near the end of her days. She told me to look in her closet for a brown paper sack. I moved a few things around to find it stuffed in the back. When I pulled the sack out of the closet, I looked inside as I carried it over to Mama.

She reached in and took out the three teddy bears that were inside.

I watched her as she straightened each of the bows tied around their necks, one blue, one red and one green.

She sat them next to her and touched each one softly.

"Daisy?", she asked as she gazed at the bears.

"Yes, Mama?", I sat next to her.

"When you find them, give them these.", she told me.

"Yes, Mama, I will.", I promised.

She continued looking at the bears, "All I ever wanted was to see them one more time.", she said as a tear rolled down her cheek.

I held her hand, "I know Mama. You will, just not how you had planned.".

Chapter Twenty-Six- (Matt)

I had looked forward to high school only because it meant I was one step closer to leaving.

Once I got there, I started skipping school and forging Dad's signature on the letters that were sent home about it.

School was the last thing on my mind when freedom was so close. One day, after being back in New Mexico again, this time, in a place longer than anywhere else we'd ever been, Dad came home carrying a newspaper. He walked straight into the kitchen where Maria was busy cooking and I was sweeping. He took it out from under his arm, unfolded it and began turning the pages quickly.

"Come over here.", he told Maria as he laid the paper out on the table and pointed to it.

She walked over to the paper and leaned in to get a closer look at what he was pointing at. She looked back at Dad with her eyebrows down, "Who's seen it?", she asked him.

He shook his head, "I'm not sure.".

"We knew this would happen. I'll call Tony.", she told him.

He nodded, "Okay, I'll get things ready.".

What is in the paper? Who is Tony?, I thought as I swept the kitchen floor pretending not to listen.

I swept my way closer to the table to try and sneak a look at what they were so concerned about, but just as I got close enough, Dad closed the newspaper and picked it up off the table to tuck back under his arm.

He went over to the phone and called his boss to let him know he wouldn't be in to work the next day. Then, he went with the paper still under his arm to his bedroom where I could hear him moving things around.

Maria finished cooking and then went to the phone. As I began wiping the table, getting it ready for supper, she snapped her fingers at me and pointed towards my room.

I left the kitchen and instead of going to my room, plopped down on the couch in the living area. I picked up a magazine from the side table and began flipping through it trying to look busy as I listened in on her conversation.

"Tony? Ciao...", she said, "Are you still needing help at the factory?".

She paused, saying nothing for a little bit then, "Yes, we can be there this weekend.", she told the person she was talking to, "Okay...okay...yes, I will call you. Grazie.".

I had no idea what she could be talking about as she hung up the phone.

When I got home from school the next day, once again the trailer was attached to the car and our furniture, along with boxes, were piled on to it.

Great, here we go again., I thought as I went up to the front door. When I stepped inside, boxes were all over the house. Dad handed me a trash bag and told me to put all my clothes in it.

"We're leaving again?", I asked him as I took the trash bag. Marc and Mitch came out of the bedroom carrying trash bags full of clothes.

Dad didn't answer me so I tried a different question, "Where are we going?".

"Would you quit asking questions and do what I tell you?", he hollered out.

I stomped off mad to my room and started throwing clothes into the trash bag. When I came out with the bag full of clothes, I pushed Marc as he walked back past me, "Hey!", he tried to push me back but missed.

Then, Mitch walked past me so I shoved him into the wall.

As he fell against the wall he cried out, "Hey! What did I do?".

I threw down the bag and stomped over to Dad, "I'm not a little kid anymore. I'm almost seventeen. Why can't you tell me where we're going?", I asked with my hands out.

Dad threw his hand in the air, "New York. We're going to New York. Now, be the man you think you are and get to work.".

"New York? Why?", I wanted to know.

Dad walked towards me, getting in my face, chest to chest, "Nunya.", he spoke quietly as we stared each other down, "Don't cross me, boy.".

Maria stepped up behind him with her arms crossed, glaring at me.

Knowing this was a battle I couldn't win, I huffed at him and reached down for the bag of clothes, slinging it over my shoulder. I walked away, keeping my eyes glued to him in anger as I carried the bag out to the car.

On the way to New York, we stopped in Michigan to visit Uncle Joe and Aunt Bess, who we hadn't seen since we left. We met them at a diner for breakfast where Aunt Becky joined us. She was no longer the teenager I had remembered her to be, instead, she was now a confident, grown woman. When she came in she awed at how much me and my brothers had grown. Together again, we all sat around the table with everyone catching up and telling stories about their time apart, everyone except us boys who kept quiet.

A waitress wearing a burgundy apron came by to take everyone's order. While Maria and Dad were ordering, Aunt Becky turned to me, "How are you, kid?", she whispered as she continued glancing at the menu in her hands.

I nodded, "Okay, I guess.", I whispered back as I rubbed my shaved head.

She looked over the top of her menu at Marc and Mitch asking the same, "What about you two?".

They looked up at Aunt Becky then took turns looking towards where Maria was sitting, still ordering.

Marc smiled, "I missed you.", was all he said. Mitch laid his menu down, "Yeah, I missed you, too.".

Aunt Becky stared deep into each of our tired eyes as if she could hear what we were thinking.

Just then, Uncle Joe announced to the waitress that we were all on his ticket as he looked down the table at us boys, "You guys get whatever you want...on me.", he smiled. The three of us looked at each other excitedly, we couldn't remember being treated so important. We looked back at him to make sure we heard him correctly as he nodded, "Go on, get what you want. Make it something good.".

We each scarfed down every bit of food on our plates as Uncle Joe teased, "You boys act like you haven't eaten in weeks.".

By the time we left the diner, my belly was so full I thought it would bust. Uncle Joe patted each of us boys on the backs as we walked to the parking lot, "Hold on now, I think I have something for you young men.", he said as he reached into his back pocket and pulled out his wallet.

Maria interrupted, putting her hand over his, "Oh, no, no, they can't accept that.", she told him.

Uncle Joe continued to open his wallet and stared at her, "My money. My nephews.", he calmly said to her, flashing a smile.

Waving her off, "Now, where was I?", as he began pulling bills out of his wallet, "Oh, yes, that's right.", he looked up at us.

"Okay, put out your hands.", he directed. As we each put out our hands, he stopped to notice the markings of scars on each of them in different places, some short and some long, each telling a different story. He looked up into each of our eyes and shook his head as if he was apologizing to us.

He began laying bills into our hands, passing them out, "This is for your birthdays.", he said as he passed out five dollar bills, "This is for Christmas.", he passed out another round of bills, "This is for your grades.", he passed out another round of bills and cleared his throat, chuckling, "Don't worry, I don't look at grades. I just know you got some.". Aunt Becky and Aunt Bess giggled.

He passed out another round of bills, this time twenties, "And this is just because.". He winked at us as he put his wallet back in his pocket.

He leaned in to whisper, "Now, listen, come gather around.", he huddled us up with his arms around us then glanced over his shoulder at Dad and Maria. He whispered into the huddle, "Don't spend it all in one place...or...do...it doesn't matter.", he smiled as he continued, "Hide it somewhere if you need to and before you run out, look on the twenty. You'll see a phone number written down, should you need it.", he patted the tops of our shaved heads and broke the huddle.

We each put the money in our pockets as Uncle Joe went over to talk to Dad and Maria. Aunt Bess gave us each a hug and told us how good it was to see us. Aunt Becky did the same and then opened my hand to slip a folded piece of paper into it, "Shhh...", she looked around, "Call me when you can.". I nodded and turned to get in the car with my brothers.

Dad and Maria joined us in the car and as we began to pull away from the diner, Maria looked back at us, "Don't you all start thinking you're anything special.".

She turned back around as we continued on our long drive.

New York was different from any other place we had been. It was bigger and brighter with tall buildings and more people. It was loud and busy all the time, any time of the day. When we first got there, we stayed with Maria's brother, Tony, for a few months until Dad found us a place to stay.

Tony looked like he had stepped out of one of those old black and white gangster movies. Short and round, he wore fancy suits, usually all black, with lots of jewelry. There was a big, golden ring on just about every one of his fingers and gold chains around his neck. His hair was black and slicked in a neat part to the side of his head.

He spoke with an accent that was different than Maria's, less Italian and more New York.

Tony had let Dad work at his plexiglass factory, starting him out as a partner.

School was different in New York too. We went to a two story massive building with swarms of other kids, easy to get lost in, so that's exactly what I did. It didn't take long for me to quit going all together.

The closer I got to eighteen, the more I dreamed of freedom. I started working at the factory instead of going to school. Marc and Mitch worked there too. They'd come in right after school and start cleaning. We were the shop boys as everyone called us. We worked for free and did what we were told, cleaning and carrying things.

We didn't mind working for free, more time at the factory meant less time at home with Maria, which was pay enough for us and when Tony left the factory to Dad and Maria, she stayed busy in the office where we hardly ever saw her anymore.

When the day came that I finally turned eighteen, I made plans to join the Army. Inside the bag I packed to take, were the numbers for Uncle Joe and Aunt Becky. I had held onto them but never called them. As I looked around in my dresser for things to take, I saw the strand from the blue bag I had kept from the fire. With each move after the fire, I had carefully kept it covered in my sock drawer. I took it out and put it in my bag to take with me.

When it was finally time to leave, I went into Marc and Mitch's bedroom where they were sitting on their beds.

"When I get to where I'm going, I'll call you.", I told them as they both looked down at the floor.

"Don't worry. I won't forget you.", I added.

Mitch looked up at me, "You promise?".

I sat down on the bed beside him, "I promise.", I put my arm around him, "It won't be long before you two are out, too. Only a few more years.".

Then I looked at Marc, "You take care of Mitch, okay?", I told him.

He looked over at me, "Haven't I always?".

I stood up, "I left some of my records for you and my old comic books on my bed.".

As I walked out of their bedroom, holding my packed bag, Mitch jumped up and ran to me. He wrapped his arms around me and without saying anything else, I hugged him back. Marc got up to join in the hug.

They followed me to the front door and stood there as I got into a taxi that was waiting for me. Dad and Maria were at the factory when I left without telling them goodbye.

Eventually, Marc and Mitch followed in my footsteps. They both dropped out of school to work at the plexiglass factory until they each turned eighteen and joined the military.

I never went back home and I never spoke to Dad or Maria ever again.

The little boys my brothers and I once were, who had been tossed around for so long, had finally made it to the good part. The part where we got to decide.

Chapter Twenty-Seven-(Daisy)

Bertie and I continued searching for the boys after Mama passed away quietly.

It took some more years with many ups and downs along the way.

We had lost touch with Becky at one point, but then found her again. Becky had moved to Georgia when we were able to reach her again. Joe and Bess were still in Michigan and would give us updates as much as they could. The issue all of us had was that once the boys became men and started off on their own, they quit contacting anyone, so even Joe and Becky weren't too sure where they were.

Eventually, Joe called Bertie out of the blue to tell her that he had heard from Marc. He was still in the Air Force and living on a base.

Bertie sat in front of the phone and began dialing the number Joe had given her for Marc.

I sat with her as she waited for an answer, "Here goes nothing.", she said to me.

She looked over at me in shock as she held the phone to her ear and cleared her throat to speak, "Hello?", she started, "Am I speaking with Marc Mair?". Her mouth dropped open as she listened for a response. She sat straight up in her chair and began patting me excitedly on the knee.

I scooted in close to hear the voice on the other end of the phone as she held it out away from her ear for me to listen.

"Marc, this is your Aunt Bertie. Do you remember me?", she asked.

A deep voice with a small New York accent answered, "Aunt Bertie? I'm not sure I do remember.".

Bertie took a deep breath, "I'm your mother's sister.".

Silence on the other end made us worry he had hung up, "Marc? Are you still there?", Bertie asked.

"Yes...yes, I'm still here.", he said.

"Marc, I've been looking for you and your brothers for quite awhile.", she told him.

He spoke slowly, "You've been looking for...me?".

"Yes. I have your sister, Daisy, here with me.", she added as she glanced over at me.

"Daisy?", he said quietly.

"Yes, do you remember her?", Bertie asked.

"Of course. Yes, of course I remember her.", he answered.

My lip quivered, I couldn't believe we were talking to him and that he remembered me after all these years.

"How are you?", Bertie asked next.

"Oh, me? I'm okay...what about my mother?", he asked.

Bertie and I looked at each other, as we both knew the next thing she had to tell him, "Well...", she twirled the phone cord nervously between her fingers, "She...uh...I'm so sorry, Marc, but...she passed away.".

There was silence again on the phone, "Marc?", Bertie asked.

"When?", he whispered.

"It's been a while. About six years.", she told him.

"Oh.", was all he said.

That phone call was the beginning of the end of Mama's search. Marc began calling often to talk to Bertie. He told her stories about all the places the boys moved around to while growing up and she told him stories about Mama. He told her that Matt had landed in prison for theft and Mitch was released from the military and living near Marc. Mitch was skeptical of us at first but after Bertie started talking to Marc more and more, over time, Mitch became more interested in talking to us.

He had finally called Bertie one night and talked to her for the first time where she ended the conversation with, "Be by your phone at six o'clock tomorrow night.".

She had me come over to her house after work and call him. I nervously waited for an answer as the phone rang on the other end.

Then, a voice answered, "Hello?".

My heart raced as I began to speak, "Hi, is this Mitch?".

He cleared his throat and said, "Yes, this is him.".

Tears started filling my eyes as I said, "This is Daisy. Your sister.".

"Daisy?", he whispered over the phone.

We began talking for what ended up being hours. He told me that he always knew he had a sister but couldn't remember my name. We shared stories about ourselves and promised to call each other again before hanging up. My heart felt as though it had been somehow mended after all of these years of waiting and searching for them.

Finally, after getting to know each other a little more on the phone, we planned a reunion.

It was clear and sunny when Marc and Mitch drove a full day to meet us at a park. When a yellow Chevelle pulled into the parking lot, I stood, squinting to see if it was them. As the driver side door opened, Bertie and I put our arms around each other in anticipation. Out stepped a tall, slender man with thick brown hair and glasses. Then, a shorter man stepped out of the passenger side, with long, dark, wavy hair. The two of them walked toward us and as they got closer, I began to recognize something about the men. The way they both walked with a strut and carried their shoulders high and proud. I had seen that walk before, it was Daddy's walk. Their noses were identical with a little point to them each with a mustache and they both had deep set brown eyes. Their faces were familiar as everything, all at once, came rushing to me. Visions of Mama's brown eyes, her soft smile, the little freckles on her nose and the dimples in her cheeks.

"Bertie?", one of the men asked.

Bertie nodded and put out her arms, "Yes! And you must be Marc!", she said as he came in for a hug.

"Yes, ma'am, it's me.", he smiled as he towered over her. The other man stood behind while Marc turned to me saying, "Sis?", he smiled and opened his arms.

He stared at my face, "Wow.", he said as he continued staring.

The other man stepped up, "It's almost like looking in a mirror.", he said.

Marc turned and grabbed the other man's shoulder, "This yahoo, is my brother, Mitch.".

Mitch pulled his arm away, "Don't let this guy start his nonsense.", he joked as he came closer to me.

Marc tapped Mitch on the arm, "Man, you sure would be prettier as a girl.", he pointed to me. We all laughed as Mitch added, "I hate to admit that I agree with anything he says, but it's like you're my pretty girl twin.".

We walked around the park getting to know each other and then sat at a picnic bench. Bertie had brought a basket filled with fried chicken that we all started to eat when we decided to discuss real matters.

Mitch started the discussion first, "So why didn't our mother want us anymore?", he asked as he chewed.

Bertie and I looked at each other in confusion, "What do you mean she didn't want you?", Bertie quickly answered, "She pined over all of you as soon as your father took off with you.".

Marc and Mitch glanced at each other, "She did?", Mitch asked.

I nodded, "Yes, she searched for you until she...passed away.", I said.

Bertie went on to tell them about the divorce and them leaving Michigan and Mama trying to figure out a way to see them.

Marc and Mitch listened as we told them about their mother looking for them. They had no idea about any of it.

"We were told she didn't love us. She didn't want us anymore.", Marc said as he looked at his chicken.

Bertie reached out her hands, putting one on each of their arms, "That's just not true.", she said, looking into their eyes, "You were very much loved and wanted. She searched for you even as she was dying.".

The men stopped eating as Marc tossed a chicken bone down and looked at his hands.

Mitch put his chicken down, wiped his hands on his pants and then stood up,

"Matt knew Dad was lying to us the whole time. He knew it. But I didn't believe Matt.", he said with frustration in his voice.

Marc stood up and put his arm around Mitch's shoulder.

"No!", Mitch blurted out as he pushed Marc's arm away and walked off.

Marc sat back down as me and Bertie were unsure what to do.

"He'll be fine.", Marc said to us, "It's just that he believed Dad a little more than the rest of us and finding out everything was a lie has been hard for him. Let him go walk it off. He'll be back.", Marc said as we watched Mitch wander around. Marc turned back to us, "So, then, tell me about her. What was she like?".

I smiled and began pouring out every memory I had of Mama. I told him about her laugh and how she painted the most beautiful paintings. How she sashayed around in new dresses and loved her red lipstick. I told them everything about her and then, as Mitch came wandering back to the table to sit down I said, "She loved you every day. She worried about you and looked for you. She spoke to you. The only thing she ever wanted was to see you again.".

I stood up from the table, "Wait here. I'll be right back.", I went to the parking lot and opened the trunk of Bertie's car.

I reached in and pulled out the brown paper sack, now wrinkled and worn out from time.

As I carried the sack back over to them, I stopped and rubbed the ruby red stone hanging from my neck once worn by Nanny and then Mama.

"We did it.", I whispered.

I sat back down at the table across from Marc and Mitch and pushed the sack towards them, "These are for you.", I told them.

Marc slowly reached for the sack and looked over at Mitch. As Marc peeked inside he pulled out one of the teddy bears and lovingly looked at it. He pulled out another teddy bear and handed it to Mitch, leaving the third teddy bear in the sack.

The men held the bears in their hands just as Mama always had, straightening the bows that were tied around their necks.

"Mama carried these bears in hopes of giving them to you one day.", I told them, "She finally found you.", I said as tears filled my eyes and rolled down my cheeks. The men looked like boys as they held the little bears in their hands, Marc holding the one with a green bow and Mitch with the blue one.

Eventually, after we finished our picnic in the park, Bertie and I took them to the cemetery where Mama was buried. As we stood there by her grave, Marc and Mitch still holding the bears, that clear sunny day was interrupted with a slight breeze.

In the breeze I heard Mama whisper to me, "Thank you, baby girl.".

We stood there, the four of us, arm in arm and finally felt a peace in knowing Mama and her boys had finally made it back together. Her search for them was over.

Epilogue- (Mama)

When I think back to my time with Mike, there were many good times that we had. At first, he was such a gentleman and seemed to know just how to win my heart. I remember when he doted over me and made me feel like I was the only one in his world. He liked getting me gifts and watched closely to my response when I received them. When another man spoke even one word to me or even looked my way he got jealous, making it clear that I was his. No man in my life had ever made me feel so important, so wanted.

Once we were married, he wanted children right away. He dreamed of having many sons, so when we had three in a row he was over the moon.

When the babies started coming though, there was a gradual change with each one. At first, he complained that I spent too much time on them and not enough on him. I noticed this and tried my best to juggle between them, making sure that when he was home, my attention stayed mainly on him. Then, he began getting frustrated easier and everything I did seemed to irritate him. I tried so hard to tend to his needs and keep him happy but nothing sufficed.

By the time we were about to welcome our fourth child he started becoming more jealous, accusing me of being with other men. His time at home became less and less. It became apparent that I did not meet his expectations as a wife. The more disgruntled he became, the more I threw myself into the children, knowing there was nothing I could do to please him. Every time he came home I hoped he would come back as a changed man. I thought the more I held on and tried to show my love for him would eventually make him happy.

When I brought home a baby girl that was the end of his rope. He became disgusted with me for ruining his plans of a boys only family. That's when he quickly changed from irritated to irrational.

Every single thing meant something bigger in his eyes. One look this way or that, even one single word would send him over the edge where he would plummet into a man I didn't know.

The only way I could contain him was to leave and give him time to cool off. It seemed to work each time when he would come back to get me, begging me to forgive him and tell me he would change. Although each time I believed him less and less, I still held onto hope that one day he would mean it.

Divorce was a last resort option in my mind so when he served me with papers, I was taken aback.

When he held my children hostage from me was when my mind immediately changed about him. It wasn't until then that I was able to truly see him for who he was.

He knew that was the last thing he could do to punish and annihilate me for my lack of trying as hard as he needed me to.

Being a mother was the single most important and cherished thing in my life and he knew it.

I never knew I could love someone so much until I became a mother. When I looked into each set of those brown eyes for the first time I fell in love all over again, each time. I was the luckiest woman in the world to feel it four times.

Watching those little babies grow brought me so much more joy than I ever even knew existed.

If only I had known our time would be cut so short, I would have hugged them even more, spent more time laughing than crying and held them tighter.

They were my drive, my hope. With the loving support of my own mother, I was able to stay focused on the task, even when I lost myself in it all, she was there to help me get back on track.

She taught me to push harder, to fight until I didn't think I could anymore and then to get back up and fight some more. I learned that I was not only fighting for my children, but also for me, Mabel. I realized that my mother was fighting her own battle as well, which was for her own children.

The only thing that kept me going besides my mother was my sweet girl who didn't know she was holding me up. When I fell, she was the motivation I needed to continue on. Her hope in me kept my flame burning and the hope of seeing my boys again one day was all I needed to stay in the fight a little longer.

In the end, baby girl was right, I wouldn't see them again in the way I had planned. I would see them again in a much different way. A much greater way than I imagined. My whispers to them all those years ago continued through them and now, today, through their children and their children's children. In those moments when they have begun to lose hope, I am the spark that continues to whisper in their ear, "Get up. Keep fighting.".

Did you love *Searching For Her Boys: A Search For Hope*? Then you should read *The Belly of the Whale*[1] by Tenise Cook!

As a young farm girl, Bonnie, lives through tragedy when her younger brother dies in a fire.

Just as Jonah from the Bible did, she learns how to continue her faith in God with the help of her family.

This journey through heartbreak and hope in small town living is set in the 1940's and is captivated from stories passed down and based on true life experiences.

1. https://books2read.com/u/badvY6

2. https://books2read.com/u/badvY6

Also by Tenise Cook

The Belly of the Whale
Searching For Her Boys: A Search For Hope

About the Author

Tenise Cook is a Texas teacher and mother who enjoys writing about her own true life experiences, as well as, those told by family members.

Her passion and faith drive her journey to share stories for others to hear, relate and hopefully encourage.

Milton Keynes UK
Ingram Content Group UK Ltd.
UKHW010848280324
440101UK00001B/94